BEFORE THE RAVENS FELL

RAVENS
BOOK 0

RYEN SANTANA

ALSO BY RYEN SANTANA

Fantasy:

The Ravens of London (Ravens, #1)

The Mourning Star (Ravens, #2)

Before The Ravens Fell (Ravens, #0)

Luminary (A Veil of Twilight, #1)

Standalone Horror:

Aegir-7

Sanguine

Theorem

Follow along on my instagram or subscribe to my newsletter for more information on releases!

And don't forget to leave a review!

www.ryenwrites.io

@ryenwrites

"There is always some madness in love. But there is also always some reason in madness."

— FRIEDRICH NIETZSCHE

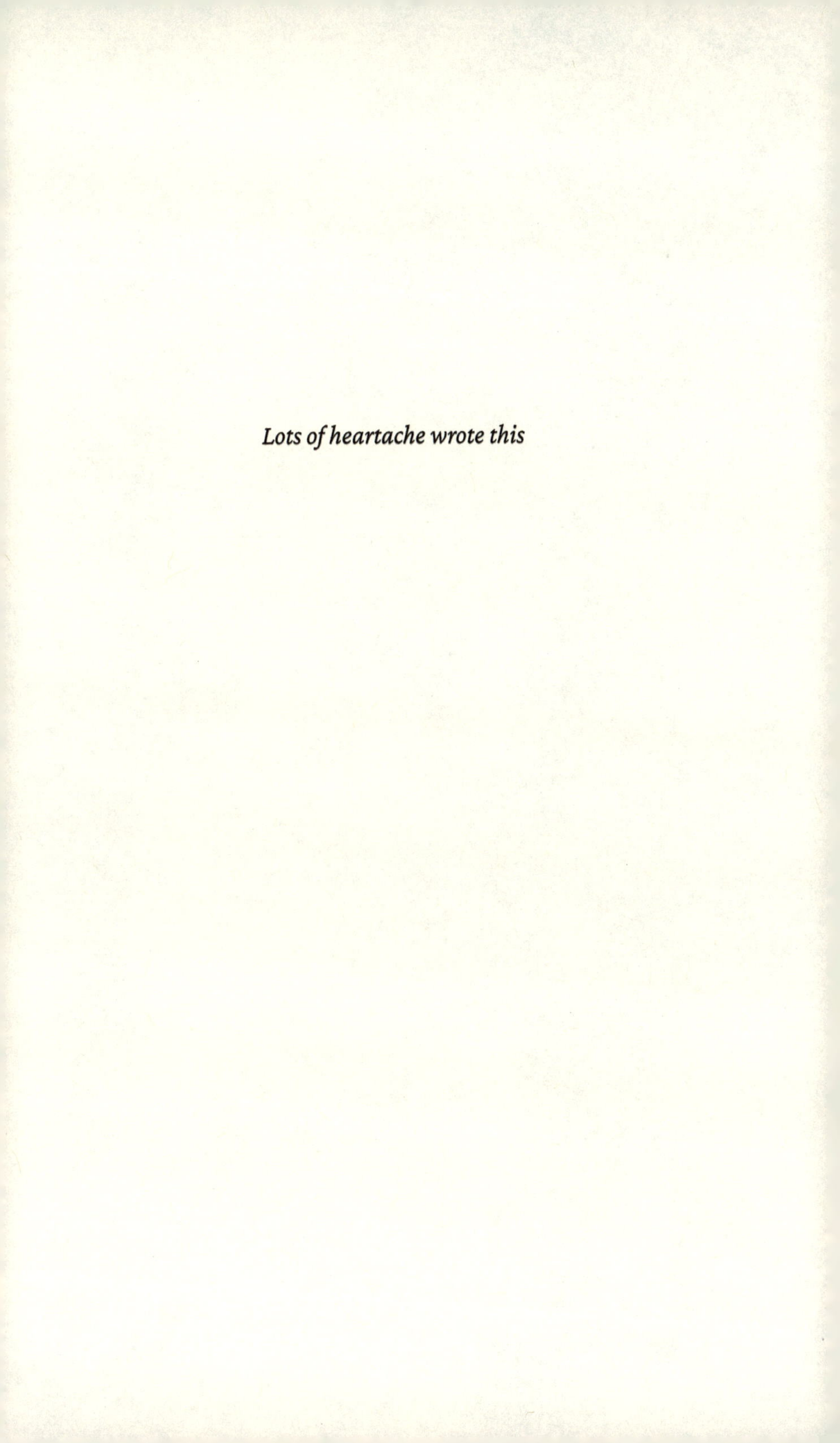

Lots of heartache wrote this

1

The night the gods came to court, the sky burned with silver fire.

Moonlight spilled through the glass dome of the Seelie palace, a molten flood that turned crystal chandeliers and floating lanterns into a universe of cold, shifting stars.

Each facet of cut glass threw a tiny blade of light across the marble floor, so the whole ballroom seemed to breathe and pulse, constellations born and dying with every faint current of air.

The scent of winter roses climbed from the garlands wound around every pillar—sweet, almost cloying, underlaid with something heavier. Magic so dense it shimmered in the lungs, coating the back of the throat like frost on iron. Mortals would have swayed on their feet. Even I felt it settle behind my ribs, a pressure that made each breath feel borrowed.

It was supposed to be beautiful.

It was supposed to be peace.

The Accord of Silent Moons had lasted three centuries. Tonight was meant to mark its renewal. The fae and the gods, gathered beneath one roof, smiling at each other with the sharp, white sincerity of wolves at a feast. Three hundred years of careful distance, of messages carried by envoys who never quite met each other's eyes, collapsed now into a single room filled with too many teeth and not enough trust.

I stood on the dais with my father, a crown pressing down on my head until the metal bit into the soft skin above my temples. I could feel the individual points of each tine, tiny crescents of pressure that would leave pale indentations long after I removed it. The weight sat just behind my brow, constant, dull, an ache I had learned never to reach up and adjust.

"Stand straighter, Ottilie" Oberon murmured. His jaw barely moved. His gaze stayed fixed on the ballroom floor, cataloguing every face below us with the patient efficiency of a predator counting a herd.

I was already standing straight. My spine had been forced into its elegant shape for years—hands folded against the small of my back during lessons, a thin rod of rowan wood balanced between my shoulder blades until my muscles memorized the posture and held it without thought. Trained into something unbending and flawless. A princess could never slouch. A future queen could never fidget, could not shift her weight from one foot to the other, could not show a single fault or fracture—not even the twitch of a finger against the heavy brocade of her skirts.

So I did as I'd been taught: hands folded at my waist, each finger placed precisely over the next, chin level with the floor, mouth curved in a smile I had practiced in mirrors until I could hold it for hours without the muscles in my cheeks trembling.

The ballroom below glittered like a promise.

Courtiers drifted through the light in gowns of moon-silk that rippled like water when they moved, catching the lantern glow and releasing it in slow, pearlescent waves. Some wore cloaks of living butterfly wings that opened and closed in lazy rhythm, shedding faint trails of iridescent dust. Jackets stitched with constellations—real ones, the thread enchanted so tiny points of starlight drifted across the fabric in their ancient patterns. Hair woven with glowing flowers that lit their wearers' faces in soft halos of amber and violet, petals warm to the touch, leaving the faint smell of honeysuckle wherever they passed. Music floated above it all from instruments I couldn't see, a harp that sounded like rain on still water, a flute made of bird bone, something low and resonant that vibrated in the soles of my shoes—delicate, bright, impossible.

Everything shone.

Everything lied.

Beneath the perfume and the enchanted light, I could smell the sharper notes: the metallic tang of wards humming in the walls, the acrid bite of defensive spells layered into the floor tiles, the faint sourness of nervous sweat that no amount of glamour could entirely conceal. A lord near the fountain laughed too loudly, his fingers white around the stem of his glass. Two ladies whispered behind their fans, their smiles frozen in place, eyes tracking the doors.

I had stood through hundreds of these nights, each an endless performance, everyone forgetting themselves behind the mask. The same choreography of bows and pleasantries, the same careful positioning—who stood near whom, who turned their back, who offered their left hand instead of their right. But tonight felt worse. Tonight the wards buzzed louder, the laughter rang thinner, and the space between every smile stretched a fraction wider.

Tonight, the gods were here.

The ballroom doors crashed open, the sound rolling

through the glass dome like thunder trapped in a bell jar. The chandeliers swayed. A shower of tiny light-motes scattered from the nearest lanterns, drifting down like disturbed snow.

Music stuttered—the harp struck a discordant note, held it, then went silent. The flute cut off mid-phrase.

Conversation crumbled into whispers that spread outward from the doors in a visible wave, heads turning, bodies stiffening, hands dropping to sides or pressing flat against stomachs.

The gods entered.

They were taller than fae, broader, their presence bending the air as if gravity had chosen sides. The floating lanterns nearest the doorway dipped toward them, drawn by some invisible weight, their flames flickering blue at the edges. Power clung to them, old and wild, a raw magic that predated faerie courts and all their tricks. I could feel it from the dais—a low hum in my teeth, a tightness across my skin like the moment before a storm breaks. The winter roses in the nearest garlands curled inward, petals closing as if in self-defense.

Three led the way.

Alistair Ravenscroft, the eldest, moved with the inevitability of a storm. Each step landed with a deliberateness that suggested the floor existed only because he permitted it. His hair caught the lanternlight, copper blazing, each strand seeming to hold its own ember. His face was carved in stone— a broad jaw that didn't move, a mouth set in a line so precise it might have been drawn with a ruler, eyes that swept the room the way a general surveys a field before battle. He didn't look at anyone in particular. He looked at everyone at once.

Nora, the youngest, walked at his side, half a step behind and to his left—a position that could have been deference but felt more like a flanking maneuver. She was beautiful like a winter star, all silver hair falling in a straight, unbroken sheet past her shoulders, cold eyes the color of lake ice at dawn. Her gown was pale and severe, catching the light without warmth. Her smile sat perfectly on her face, the kind of smile that never reached the muscles around her eyes, as sharp as a knife concealed behind her back. When she passed a cluster of fae courtiers, two of them stepped backward without seeming to realize they'd moved.

And then—the third.

Calum Ravenscroft.

The name was already in my mind before anyone could whisper it, rising unbidden from years of bedtime warnings and council briefings and my father's voice, tight with something I had never quite been able to name.

The God of Nightmares.

I'd grown up with stories about him, as if he were a shadow always at my heels: cruel, unpredictable, chaos with a face. The kind of stories told to fae children who wouldn't sleep—*behave, or Calum Ravenscroft will find you in your dreams.* Alistair was controlled, Nora was calculating, but Calum— Calum was the one the stories never quite agreed on. A monster. A madman. A force that enjoyed destruction the way others enjoyed music.

I expected a monster.

Instead, he looked like a man who'd stepped into a masque he meant to ruin. He entered behind his siblings but separate from them, a deliberate gap of several feet, as though proximity were a concession he hadn't agreed to make. He stood at the edge of the crowd, tall even among the gods, black hair cropped short enough to show the hard line of his jaw and the sharp architecture of his skull. His eyes were so pale they looked almost colorless—blue grey bleeding into silver bleeding into something that caught the moonlight pouring through the dome and threw it back, flat and unreadable. His clothing was plain: a dark coat that hung open, the fabric good but unadorned, an open collar showing the hollow of his throat and the edge of a collarbone, nothing jeweled, nothing embroidered. Among the glittering court, he looked like a smudge of charcoal on a painted canvas.

He didn't bow.

He didn't smile.

While everyone else bent into their roles—spines curving, heads dipping, mouths arranging themselves into the proper shapes of welcome—Calum Ravenscroft only watched. His gaze moved across the room slowly, the way a blade moves across a whetstone, and wherever it landed, something in the air seemed to tighten and hold still.

And I found I couldn't look away. My carefully trained posture held, my smile stayed fixed, but my eyes refused to obey, tracking him the way a compass needle tracks north— involuntary, insistent, as if some mechanism deeper than training had locked into place.

"Daughter."

Oberon's voice sliced through my thoughts, low and precise, the verbal equivalent of a hand closing around a wrist.

"Yes, Father."

"Stop staring."

I'd been caught. Heat crept up the back of my neck and spread to my cheeks—I could feel it, bright and damning, and I forced my eyes back to the crowd below, fixing them on a courtier's glowing hair ornament with desperate concentration.

"Forgive me."

Oberon made a sound, low and warning, barely more than a vibration in his chest. His fingers, resting on the arm of his throne, pressed down until the tendons in his hand stood out like harp strings.

"Remember who you are tonight."

The Seelie heir. The court's perfect symbol. The woman who would rule. I knew every word of it—had heard it repeated so many times the syllables had worn smooth, like river stones, losing their meaning through sheer repetition.

Still, my gaze slipped back before I could stop myself, drawn by the same maddening gravity that pulled the lanterns toward the gods.

Calum had moved. He stood by a servant with silver trays of wine—a boy, young, whose hands shook so badly the glasses chimed faintly against each other like tiny bells. Calum took a glass without looking at the trembling boy, his fingers closing around the stem with an ease that suggested he'd done this a thousand times at a thousand events he hadn't wanted to attend, and drained half of it in a single swallow.

His face made it clear the wine was a disappointment. His mouth tightened at one corner—not a grimace, exactly, but a subtle contraction of muscle, the way someone's face shifts when they've bitten into fruit and found it mealy. He looked at the glass as though it had personally offended him, then drank the rest anyway.

There was something about the way he did it. The utter lack of pretense—no performance, no acknowledgment of the hundred eyes that tracked his every movement. He didn't hold the glass elegantly. He didn't savor the wine. He didn't arrange his expression for an audience. The way he ignored the watching eyes sparked something sharp in me, something that sat just beneath my sternum and pulled, a hook I hadn't known was there.

He looked bored.

Utterly, exquisitely bored.

This was the most delicate night in centuries, a peace balanced on a blade's edge, every word and gesture freighted with the weight of potential war—and Calum looked as if he'd been dragged to a dull supper and was counting the minutes until he could leave. He leaned one shoulder against the wall beside the window, crossed his ankles, and held his empty glass loosely at his side, the posture of a man waiting for something worth his attention and not expecting to find it.

"Impressive restraint," Nora murmured behind him. I caught it only because the acoustics of the dome carried certain frequencies with treacherous clarity—her voice arrived at the dais thin but intact, like a whisper pressed between pages.

I didn't catch Calum's answer, only saw the faint curl of his mouth—one side lifting, slow and private, a smile meant for no one but himself.

Then Oberon began to speak.

He rose from his throne, and the motion was its own kind of magic—unhurried, absolute, the way a mountain would rise if mountains chose to move. His voice filled the hall without effort, warm and commanding, resonant enough to vibrate in the glass overhead. He welcomed the gods. He spoke of harmony. Of a future built on shared purpose, on the wisdom of the Accord, on the strength that came from unity between ancient powers. His hands moved in careful, measured gestures, each one rehearsed, each one designed to convey openness and authority in equal measure.

I'd heard variations of this speech since childhood— standing in this same spot, wearing smaller crowns that pressed into the same tender places, watching the same practiced movements.

Tonight it sounded like someone insisting there was no fire as they doused the room in oil. Each word of peace fell into the silence and dissolved, leaving nothing behind, and beneath the soaring rhetoric I could hear what wasn't being said—the careful omission of border disputes, of stolen magic, of fae who had vanished in god territory and gods who had been found dead in ours.

Applause rolled over the ballroom, a wave of sound that crested and broke against the dome. It was enthusiastic and hollow, the kind of applause that comes from hands moving because they're supposed to, not because they want to.

The servants returned, wine and glowing fae liquors on their trays—drinks that shifted color as you tilted them, that tasted of starlight or autumn or the memory of a first kiss, depending on who held the glass. Music swelled again, the unseen instruments finding their rhythm, layering melody over melody until the air itself seemed to hum. The night resumed its performance.

I should have remained on the dais, statue-still beside my father, hands folded, spine perfect, smile fixed.

Instead, I stepped into the crowd.

The descent from the dais was seven steps. I counted each one, feeling the silk of my gown drag against the marble, hearing the faint whisper of fabric that sounded, absurdly, like a held breath being released.

A princess walking among her court was unremarkable; the courtiers parted as if I carried a blade, bodies shifting to either side in a practiced choreography of deference that opened a corridor of empty space wherever I moved. They bowed, curtsied, sang my praises—*Your Highness, you are radiant, Your Highness, the crown suits you, Your Highness, what an honor.* Mouths moved. Eyes calculated. I returned their words without thinking, the responses worn into grooves so deep they required no conscious thought, my lips forming the shapes of gratitude while my mind was already ten steps ahead, already across the room.

My attention was elsewhere.

Calum stood at the far edge of the ballroom, near a

window that overlooked the gardens drowned in moonlight. The glass beside him was fogged faintly where the warmth of the room met the cold radiating off the panes, and beyond it I could see the pale geometry of hedgerows and fountains rendered ghostly and strange by the silver light. He had acquired a second glass of wine—or perhaps a third—and held it loosely, his thumb tracing an absent circle on the rim.

He was alone.

Watching.

Drinking.

A wolf forced to sit among lambs, one shoulder still pressed to the wall, his body angled toward the room but not part of it, barely containing his contempt for the game. Every few seconds his gaze would track across the crowd, pause on something—a too-loud laugh, a too-deep bow—and his jaw would tighten, almost imperceptibly, before moving on.

I slowed as I drew near. My footsteps, which had been purposeful, became measured. I was aware of my hands, my posture, the exact angle of my chin. I was aware that I was being watched—not just by him, but by every pair of eyes that had tracked my path across the floor and was now holding its breath.

Up close, the air shifted. It grew heavier, denser, charged with a pressure that prickled against my skin like the static before lightning—a crawling sensation across my forearms, the fine hairs at the back of my neck rising. My lungs worked harder, as though the air near him contained something thicker than oxygen. The winter roses pinned to the nearest pillar had gone completely still, their petals clenched tight as fists.

He saw me before I spoke.

His eyes lifted from his glass, met mine. Up close, they were almost blinding—not beautiful, exactly, but overwhelming, the pale grey-silver of them catching every source of light in the room and refracting it back with an intensity that made me want to blink and look away. I didn't. Something stubborn in me refused.

"Princess," he said, voice low and dry, the word stripped of all ceremony. "Shouldn't you be somewhere more ceremonial?"

Not rude. Not polite, either. Somewhere precisely in between, balanced on an edge that suggested he knew exactly where the line was and enjoyed standing on it.

A smile fought its way to my lips—a real one, not the practiced version, and I could feel the difference in my own face, the way it pulled at different muscles, sat in a different place.

"Shouldn't you?"

He glanced down at his wine. Turned the glass a quarter rotation in his fingers.

"Apparently not."

He looked back at me, and something shifted in his expression—a sharpening, the boredom receding like a tide to reveal something alert and watchful underneath. Interest tightening the lines around his eyes, pulling his focus into a point that I could feel land on me like a physical weight.

"You look miserable," I said.

He blinked. It was the first unguarded movement I'd seen him make—a single, reflexive flutter of surprise that broke through the careful indifference like a crack in a wall.

"I am at a fae ball," he said after a pause, and the pause was just long enough to suggest he'd considered and discarded several other responses before settling on this one. "Misery feels appropriate."

I laughed.

It escaped before I could restrain it—bright and sharp in the perfumed air, loud enough that two courtiers near the window turned their heads. I felt it leave my body like something uncaged, felt the careful architecture of my composure shift and resettle around the gap it left. My hand rose halfway to my mouth before I stopped it, forced it back to my side.

The music played on, the court shimmered, the three-hundred-year peace hung in the air like spun glass—beautiful, intricate, and so fragile that a single wrong vibration could shatter it into a thousand pieces.

But for the first time all night, I felt something dangerously close to real amusement. It sat warm in my chest, unfamiliar and reckless, and I recognized it the way you recognize a language you haven't spoken in years—distantly, with a pang.

Calum Ravenscroft tilted his head, studying me as if I'd surprised him. His eyes narrowed slightly, not with suspicion but with a kind of recalibration—the look of someone who has made an assumption and is in the process of discarding it. The corner of his mouth shifted, not quite a smile, but the architecture of one, the foundation being laid.

"Careful," he said quietly. The word dropped between us like a stone into still water.

"Why?"

He raised his glass, slow and mocking, a toast to no one and nothing, the gesture carrying the weight of something he wasn't saying.

"Because," he said, "I suspect this conversation is the moment everything begins to go very wrong."

The glass dome above us caught the moonlight and held it, trembling. Somewhere in the ballroom, a winter rose opened, its petals unfurling against all reason, releasing a scent like cold metal and smoke.

And I believed him.

2

———————

I should have left him there.

My mother's voice echoed in the recesses of my mind for situations just like this—*move on, keep walking, let your hem brush the floor and your eyes see nothing.* Twenty-seven years I'd spent absorbing her lessons, each one a shard of knowledge on how to navigate the delicate tapestry of court life: how to smile without baring too much, how to nod without bending. I was well-versed in the arithmetic of grace and the calculus of pauses; every moment lingered cost dearly, with the court collecting its due in silence and scrutiny.

Yet my feet had betrayed me, and against my better judgment, I stopped.

Calum Ravenscroft stood in the shadows of the third window along the eastern wall, framed by the arching panes that overlooked the moon-swallowed gardens. He was leaning —or perhaps more accurately, positioned with precision— against a marble column, the angelic indifference of his posture suggesting he'd commanded every angle, every inch, to serve his nonchalance. His arms hung loosely across his chest, the toe of one boot crossed over the other, its scuffed leather a silent rebellion against the court's tailored perfection. He seemed at ease, as if the entire Seelie court had performed its grand pageantry one too many times for his liking.

The faelight flirted with his features, painting them in strokes of light and shadow—illuminating the sharp contours of his cheekbones and the resolute line of his jaw, where a muscle twitched as if suppressing a rogue thought. A faint scar arced upward from his temple, as slender as a spider's thread, disappearing into the inky waves of his hair just above his ear. In the fractured light, he seemed an entity of duality: half cast in golden warmth, half enveloped in enigmatic darkness.

He wasn't the monster from my childhood tales, those woodcut demons with twisted spines and hands like blades. No claws, no pulsating veins, just a man—tall, dark-haired, his locks curling stubbornly at his collar, defying every attempt at discipline. His coat was a midnight ocean, the fabric drinking in light, buttoned to his throat while everyone else flaunted jeweled necklines like proud peacocks. Yet his stillness made the revelers around him appear frantic—a stone in a river that neither shifts nor can be overlooked.

And that alone made him dangerous.

A danger that crept upon you silently, unnoticed until it was too late.

"You're staring again," Calum observed, his voice low and deliberate as he lifted a wine glass that remained untouched. The wine's surface captured the faelight, shivered briefly, then returned to stillness. He brought the glass to his lips, but they remained closed around the rim. It struck me then that he hadn't drunk all evening. The glass was merely an accessory, a tool for his hands to avoid the question of their emptiness.

"You were staring first."

"Observation." His gaze fixed on mine, heavy and unflinching, the grey depths of his eyes catching a flicker of light that rendered them momentarily luminous. It was a gaze that immobilized, that made you acutely aware of your own smallness—not in stature, for I stood taller than many ladies of the court—but small in the way a mouse feels beneath a hawk's shadow. Intense. Calculated.

"Staring," I repeated, though my voice felt oddly fragile, caught in the swell of music and murmur of conversation around us.

His smile was a crooked thing, tugging at the scarred side of his mouth, an expression that seemed to cost him something, as though his face had made a decision without his consent.

"Princess," he murmured, the title weighted differently than when uttered by others—neither reverent nor scornful, but possessive, as one might refer to a place visited once and never quite left behind, "if I intended to stare, you would be aware."

The word *aware* resonated between us, a vibration that hummed through my bones, cold at first—a frost running its fingers down my spine—then warm, unfurling from my core, settling at the base of my skull. I dismissed it, adjusted my sleeve—a reflexive gesture honed since childhood—and kept my breathing steady, the way my etiquette tutor had drilled it into me until it became second nature.

"Confident words for someone standing in an adversary's court."

"Adversary?" His gaze drifted briefly, taking in the assembled courtiers. Silk whispered against silk, laughter tinkling falsely like glass about to break. A cough stifled and a compliment exaggerated. "I thought we were here to celebrate peace."

"That's the official narrative."

"And the unofficial one?"

My eyes roved over the ballroom, truly seeing it through fresh perspective—how the fae chandeliers dripped with honeyed light that pulsed like a living heartbeat, cloaking imperfections with a deceptive glow. The walls adorned in green and gold, the stag and oak of our banners breathing with light. Near the entrance, the offending strip of silver—a ribbon so slight it mocked the Unseelie court, an insult wrapped in protocol.

Marble floors gleamed beneath us, mirrors of the chandeliers hanging above, and the air was thick with jasmine, wax, and the faint mineral tang of magic—charms preserving the feasts, glamours hiding the truth. Here, smiles were masks, conversations fine-tuned weapons. Hands clutched crystal with whitening knuckles—a minuscule betrayal amidst a flawlessly staged performance.

"The unofficial story is that trust is absent here."

Calum took in my words, idly tracing a pattern on his glass with his thumb, a trail left clear in the condensation. His gaze swept the room: the servant's door, the shadowed alcove, the open balcony—mapping exits, counting escape routes like a man accustomed to leaving rooms quickly.

He chuckled—a soft, intimate sound that warmed the air between us and shrank the space without movement.

"There she is."

"Who?"

"The honest princess."

I opened my mouth to counter, but—

—the music stopped, not faded, severed mid-note. A violin's tremolo cut off, the harp's final note suspended, dying in the sudden void. Silence reverberated outward: dancers frozen mid-step, conversations halted, secrets smothered.

Even the candles paused, their flames still, wax falling like quiet footsteps.

At the center, a servant knelt, trembling so fiercely he seemed about to shatter. A child, barely fourteen, still growing into his frame. The wine soaked his tunic, outlining each rib in rapid rhythm. His hands pressed to the stone as if holding the world together by force of will.

Wine pooled around him, seeping into the marble's veins, staining my father's cloak—a regal garment now marred by crimson tendrils. Like blood on snow. Irreversible.

Oberon loomed above, an unyielding presence. Shoulders square, chin lifted, hands ring-adorned and still. His silence was threat enough, a predator's patience in the hunt. The room recoiled, silk whispering away from the center, leaving the boy isolated.

The servant's mouth formed silent pleas—half-words of *please* and *sorry,* tangled and trapped in panic.

My father's expression shifted, barely perceptible—a tightening of lips, a hardening of eyes, the warmth drained to a distant memory. It was a face I knew well, read like a sky predicting storms.

"You clumsy fool," Oberon said softly, the words carrying weight beyond volume, sealing fate with chilling finality.

The boy flinched under the rebuke, forehead to the floor, shoulders hitching with each breath, trying to shrink, to disappear. A lock of hair stuck to his temple, making him look heartbreakingly young.

"I'm sorry, Your Majesty—I didn't—"

Oberon struck him.

The sound cracked through the hall, flesh meeting flesh with a resounding clap that echoed between the columns, embedding itself in memory. The boy crumpled, elbow meeting marble with a dull thud, body smearing the spilled wine, the stain spreading like a living thing.

None moved.

Faces turned away, conversations hushed to nothing. A court rehearsed in seeing nothing, their expressions masks of indifference. The façade of witnessless observers.

My stomach clenched, a visceral protest, yet I stood firm, nails biting into silk, pain a focus, a reminder of the wrongness.

"Father," I spoke, stepping forward, words balanced like a blade, my voice a practiced shield.

He met my gaze with chilling precision, the gaze of a king, not a father. Words spoken out of turn hung in the air unacknowledged.

"Stay where you are, daughter."

The servant struggled to rise, slipping on the stained marble. He winced in pain, determination etched into his young features, yet prepared to use his own clothing to mend his mistake.

Oberon's grip tightened, lifting the boy, choking him with his own collar. The child hung, feet searching in vain, hands too afraid to grasp for aid.

"Disrespect isn't erased with a rag," Oberon said, his tone deceptively soft, twisting tenderness into cruelty.

"It was an accident," I said, voice steady despite the roil inside, every instinct screaming to act but remaining still, poised, controlled.

He ignored me.

"Accidents expose incompetence."

The boy trembled, blood trailing from his mouth, merging with the wine in a scarlet testament.

"Please—"

Oberon's fist hung in the air, trembling with restrained

fury as candlelight fractured around the gemstones adorning his knuckles. The servant shuddered, anticipating pain that hadn't yet arrived, his body instinctively curling inward. The court was impeccably still, the kind of stillness practiced over years by those who understood precisely when to avert their gaze.

And then, a voice sliced through the silence.

"What does this achieve?"

The sound emerged from behind me.

Soft.

Lethal.

It expanded like ink in water, spreading slowly, seeping into every corner of the room before anyone thought to breathe.

Calum moved past my shoulder before I could hold him back. His sleeve brushed against my arm as he glided by, and a jolt of something cold and electrifying raced across my skin. He walked as if the world existed to accommodate him, every step unhurried, exuding the assured confidence of a predator in its domain.

The court collectively took a breath. Silk and brocade whispered as bodies shifted ever so slightly, and a glass clattered loudly on marble in the distance.

Amusement played on his lips, a ghost of a smile that could be mistaken for courtesy by those who missed the deadened stare in his eyes.

"You're letting a minor accident disrupt a perfectly fine evening," he addressed Oberon. His gaze flicked briefly to the dark stain blooming across the marble, the spilled wine threading itself between the tiles like a living thing. The servant trembled, wine droplets still trickling from his fingertips.

The room seemed to constrict, the grandeur of the Seelie ballroom—its vaulted ceilings and moonstone-wrapped columns—drawing tight around the two of them like a closing hand.

Oberon turned with calculated leisure, releasing the servant just enough to pivot, his robes whispering against the floor, his golden circlet aglow under the floating chandeliers. His expression held the kind of blankness I had learned to dread more than any anger.

"Mind your words," Oberon warned, his voice frostier than the room, chilling the air around us. "You stand in my court."

"And still," Calum replied, eyes resting on the boy in Oberon's grip—a lad barely sixteen, livery soaked, a line of blood tracing his chin to his throat—"you feel compelled to demonstrate your power."

A ripple passed through the crowd. I saw it physically in the way people leaned back, how hands clutched chair arms, and how courtiers near the front subtly retreated an inch without even realizing.

I could almost hear Alistair mutter a curse behind me, his hand instinctively gripping the pommel of a blade forbidden within the palace walls.

"Boy," Oberon spat.

The word landed like a physical strike.

Calum's demeanor shifted at once. Amusement drained from his face as swiftly as dusk overcomes daylight, leaving behind a vast, empty expanse. A flash of something dangerous crossed his eyes, sharp and quick, as though a blade had been unsheathed and hidden again in a single heartbeat. He inclined his head slightly, muscles tense, the air around him tightening, vibrating with the promise of violence.

Instinct propelled me forward.

"Father," I interjected, stepping between them.

Silk gathered at my ankles as I moved, Calum's warmth a

steady presence at my back, sending the fine hairs on my neck tingling. Oberon's gaze fixed on me—ancient, pale green, sharp enough to cut.

My hand settled gently on Calum's arm.

Heat surged beneath my palm. Not the warmth of comfort —this was heat that throbbed, that pulsed, like pressing against a furnace knowing what lay behind the door. His forearm was steel beneath the fabric of his sleeve, drawn taut, a bowstring on the brink of snapping.

"Please."

For a heartbeat, the room held its breath. The music had stopped unnoticed, and the silence was the kind that listened, that waited. Somewhere, wax dripped steadily onto marble, a metronome in the quiet.

Oberon examined me. His scrutiny felt clinical, as though determining the flaw in a gemstone. I maintained my façade, my breathing measured. I'd perfected this mask against fear since childhood.

Then he released the servant.

His fingers unfurled slowly, one by one, a deliberate act of will over concession.

The boy collapsed, knees striking marble with a grim crack that turned my stomach. He curled forward, clutching his ribs, breaths shallow and ragged—a stark reminder of lessons learned in silence.

"Remove him," Oberon commanded.

Two guards rushed forward, armor clinking softly. They lifted the trembling servant by his arms, his feet dragging, tracing thin red lines through the spilt wine. Not a sound escaped him. He knew better now.

Oberon's gaze locked on Calum.

His face bore the mask of a gracious monarch, but the vein

throbbing at his temple betrayed him. His jaw clenched tighter than necessary.

"This court values respect," he pronounced.

Calum's smile was faint, a bare acknowledgment that sat on his mouth like a sheathed dagger—plainly visible, a threat left unspoken.

"And yet," he noted, "I've witnessed astonishingly little of it tonight."

His words dropped into the silence like pebbles into a pond, rippling outward. The Seelie ambassador exhaled sharply, and Lady Maren's fan stilled entirely.

Before Oberon could respond, I grasped Calum's wrist.

His pulse thrummed beneath my fingers. Fast. Steady. That heat radiated once more, and I caught a scent that brought to mind woodsmoke, iron, and something more enigmatic—deep woods and ancient magic, the expectant silence before a storm.

"Walk with me," I whispered.

He didn't resist.

And that might have been the most startling aspect of all. This man who had faced down the mightiest fae king across three realms, who stood at the heart of an enemy court with supreme confidence—he allowed me to lead him away without hesitation.

We traversed the ballroom under the weight of a hundred watchful eyes. I felt their gazes pressing into my back, a tangible sensation, like the pricking of needles. The crowd parted, bodies shifting aside in whispers of silk and murmured speculation. I held my head high, my movements composed, resolutely not looking back at my father.

I pushed open the balcony doors, stepping into the night.

Frigid air rushed around us, fragrant with jasmine, frost, and the distant metallic tang of the river winding through the estate. It hit my flushed skin like a shock, and I breathed deeply, expanding my lungs until they ached. The ballroom's sounds—the whispers, the stifling elegance—fell away as the doors closed behind us.

The gardens sprawled beneath us, a tableau of silver and shadow, trees rustling softly in the breeze. Moonlight spilled across cobbled paths like quicksilver, and the hedgerows cast long, angular shadows over the manicured lawns. Below, a fountain whispered secrets to the night, while pale flowers reached toward the moon.

I turned on him.

"What were you thinking?"

My voice cut sharper than intended, fraying at the edges, and I realized my hands were trembling. I clamped them against my skirts.

Calum leaned against the stone balustrade, arms crossed. He tilted his head slightly, regarding me with the detached calm of someone watching a tempest from a distance. Moonlight sculpted his features, highlighting sharp cheekbones, a strong jaw, and eyes that seemed to shift with the light—silver now, almost luminous.

"Frequently."

"You just challenged the Seelie king before his entire court."

"Indeed."

No pause. No remorse. He spoke as if confirming the obvious.

"You could have ignited a war."

He shrugged, a slight movement, the gesture of a man unconcerned with hypothetical dangers.

"Worse has begun from less."

I stared at him.

His calm infuriated me. A stray lock of dark hair fell across his forehead, swaying in the breeze, and he made no effort to move it. He stood there, leaning against my father's palace railing, as though savoring a pleasant evening.

"You don't even know that boy."

"No," he agreed.

"Then why—"

"Because," he interrupted softly, amusement stripped away, leaving something raw beneath, "men like your father relish in reminding others of their fragility."

A pang hit my chest. His words unsettled something carefully barricaded within—something bruised and familiar, something I did not wish to unearth beneath moonlight with a stranger witnessing.

"He's still the king."

"And?"

"And the treaty stands due to him."

Calum tilted his head slightly, avian in his consideration, as if seeing me anew, discovering something unexpected.

"Does it?"

His question unnerved me more than it should have. It lingered between us, small and sharp, embedding itself beneath my skin like a splinter—unnoticed at first, then impossible to disregard.

"You suggest peace is an illusion."

"I suggest peace is ephemeral."

He moved away from the railing, drawing nearer. The space between us condensed, charged with an energy that thrummed. Up close, his presence radiated a power unlike the cultivated magic of the Seelie court—golden, refined elegance. His was older, wilder, pressing against my skin like static before a storm, making my teeth ache faintly.

"Tell me honestly, Princess."

"What?"

"If the treaty dissolved tomorrow, how long do you think this court would remain standing?"

I didn't respond. The answer seemed etched in the swift shadows moving across the floor.

Not long.

Calum's gaze was a slow dance across my features, like an artist tracing each contour with deliberate intent. The torchlight from the balcony flickered over his angular face, gilding one side in amber while the other melted into ink-dark shadow.

Then, in the quiet between heartbeats, something in his expression shifted—an imperceptible softening around his eyes, a relaxation of his jaw that most wouldn't notice.

"You're exhausted," he said.

The words jolted through me like the lash of a winter wind. My fingers curled involuntarily around the stone railing— granite, cold and unyielding, leaching warmth through the silk of my gloves.

"Of what?"

"Of pretending this gilded cage grants you wings."

The gardens blurred below, dreamlike. Lanterns punctuated the hedgerows, pinpricks of light against carefully ordered paths. Everything sculpted. Everything obedient. Even the roses asked permission to climb.

"You've known me five minutes," I replied, my voice mercifully steady.

"And already I see you're gasping for breath."

His honesty was a sharp blade sliding between my ribs, lodging somewhere beneath my sternum. I swallowed, feeling the weight of my jeweled collar settle against my skin.

I forced laughter, crystalline and hollow—a sound meant to fill space without disrupting it.

"You're astute."

"You're transparent."

I leaned beside him against the railing, drawn inexplicably toward the scent of woodsmoke and pine that clung to his coat —a stark contrast to the floral haze of jasmine and rosewater entrenched in every corner of this palace. The stone was a stark chill through my sleeve. Somewhere below, a nightbird offered its song to the empty air.

"You speak boldly for someone ensconced in enemy territory."

"Enemy territory implies I intend to leave this place intact."

A genuine laugh broke free, escaping me in a rush. I bit my lip too late to recall it. His mouth twitched in response; he had noticed.

"Careful," I warned.

"Why?"

"Because you might discover joy in this madness."

He turned to face me, the movement slow, deliberate. The space between us contracted into mere inches. His eyes—grey, not the onyx I'd believed—held storms and secrets.

"And if I did?"

Something wild and defiant unfurled within me, a heat sparking at the base of my thoughts, dismantling the structure of every wall I'd so carefully built. My pulse thrummed at my throat, acutely aware his gaze could trace its path.

Something perilous.

"Then perhaps," I mused, "you should return tomorrow."

His brow lifted, a minute movement loaded with meaning.

"Tomorrow."

"Yes."

"And where might this rendezvous occur?"

I glanced toward the gardens, past the orchestrated paths and dutiful hedgerows, beyond the fountain where water sang over polished stone, past the boundary of iron gates. At the grounds' edge stood an ancient willow, its branches swaying like dancers loosed from constraint. Even from here, its movements were free, untamed—a rebellion against the pruning demands of order.

"Midnight," I offered, "beneath the willow."

Calum measured me with his gaze, searching my face for guile or the elaborate deceit of court intrigue—a door cracked open with a guard lurking behind it.

Silence stretched. The wind carried the ghost of a waltz, barely audible beneath glass and velvet.

Then a smile, slow as dawn, unfurled across his face. It began in his eyes, reaching his mouth last—an expression unguarded and true.

"Princess," he murmured, "that sounds dangerously like a dreadful plan."

"Most thrilling adventures are."

Another heartbeat passed between us. The torch beside us sputtered in the breeze, sending shadows capering across the stone. From within, the sound of crystal clinking and courtly laughter reached us like echoes from another world. Yet here, on this balcony above the gardens, reality was quietly unraveling.

He inclined his head, a gesture filled with private understanding.

"Midnight," he affirmed.

Inside, the music swelled anew. Through the doors, dancers wove intricate patterns—threads of silk catching the light, hands meeting and parting in a choreography as old as the peace it celebrated. The fragile equilibrium endured, its surface unmarred. But change whispered in the air.

I felt it in the wind's shift, bringing the scent of northern rains, his rains. In the warmth lingering on the railing where his hand had rested. In the electricity singing beneath my skin, waiting, just waiting, for lightning to strike.

I had invited the most dangerous man across three realms to meet me alone in the dark.

And for the first time in my life—

I was eager for the arrival of tomorrow.

3

All morning, Calum Ravenscroft never so much as flicked his gaze my way. No mocking grin, no heavy stare, no secret signal recalling last night's rendezvous beneath the willow. He was absurdly composed—leaning against a column in the back, shoulders squared, every limb arranged in careful nonchalance. To me it felt like his indifference pressed against my skin sharper than any look of scorn.

If moonlight whispering through the willow and the soft rattle of its leaves hadn't echoed in my mind, I might have convinced myself our midnight tryst was a dream. But as the council's argument petered out and courtiers filtered toward the exit, the hall's atmosphere snapped taut—like a bowstring pulled too tight. My spine tingled with the certainty that eyes had fallen upon me. I forced my chin higher, carried on toward the Autumn Court ambassador as if nothing had shifted, right up until nearly everyone had poured through the doorway.

That was when I finally stepped off the dais.

That was when I felt Calum's presence at my side.

"You look bored," he murmured, voice low enough that only I could hear over the distant click of marble heels.

I didn't turn. My fingertips curled around the hem of my gown. "You look insufferable."

He tilted his head, one dark eyebrow arching. "That's my natural state."

We eased into the corridor, the sun slicing through stained-glass windows and painting prisms on the glossy floor. Servants bore trays of crystal flutes and embroidered napkins, eyes glued to the stone beneath their feet. Helmets of silver-sheathed guards peered at us in passing, then looked away so fast it felt like proof they'd seen something forbidden.

"You ignored me all morning," I said, folding my arms so tightly I could almost feel the bones shift.

"I was behaving," he replied, lips curving into the smallest smirk.

"That must have been difficult."

"Excruciating," he said, and the single word sounded half-amused, half-weary.

I risked a glance. He was watching the sunlight chase itself across the floor tiles; his eyes flashed cobalt whenever the light struck them right.

"You could have acknowledged me," I pressed.

He inhaled slowly, as if tasting the marble-scented air. "And risk the entire court concluding that its princess had spent last night skulking through royal gardens with a god most consider untrustworthy?"

I squared my shoulders. "That's not what happened."

"Isn't it?"

My cheeks warmed. I swallowed hard. "You exaggerate."

He shrugged. "Princess," he said—his tone as light as a breeze in summer—"you invited me into your father's gardens at midnight."

I shot him a sharp look. "And you came."

"Yes."

"That makes us equally culpable."

"I never denied it."

We turned a corner into a quieter wing, where distant laughter faded and the hush of afternoon settled over marble arches. Golden beams spilt in through tall windows, glinting the ironwork of the railings.

"You shouldn't follow me like this," I whispered, lowering my voice even as my heart drummed against my ribs.

"You shouldn't invite gods to secret meetings," he countered, stepping closer.

"Yet here we are."

"Yet here we are."

Ahead, the terrace doors yawned open. A blast of cold air rolled down the corridor, carrying the sharp tang of frost. I slipped out past him and the gardens spread below, every hedge dusted with glittering ice and silver-blue petals nodding beneath a wintry sun. Fountains tinkled, sending thin ribbons of water into the pale light.

Calum leaned on the stone balustrade, shoulders relaxed.

"You look like you're trying very hard not to smile," he observed, voice quieter than before.

"I'm not smiling," I said, though my lips threatened to curve.

"You are."

"I'm not."

"You're terrible at lying."

His lips quirked upward. "Bold words from a god."

"I never said you were good at anything."

I tucked my hands behind me, fingertips brushing the carved griffins in the railing. The wind tugged at the skirts of my gown.

"You're impossible," I said.

He straightened, turning his gaze outward. "And yet you keep meeting me."

I bristled. "I didn't say that."

"You didn't need to."

He waved a hand toward the garden paths winding into the misty treeline. "You chose a new spot today."

"I didn't choose anything."

"You walked straight here."

"I come here often."

"Do you?" He let the question hang, and I felt the air thicken.

"Yes," I admitted.

"With strange gods trailing behind?"

"That part's new."

He let out a soft chuckle, surprising me with its warmth. I stayed silent, listening to the faint jingle of armor as guards paced near the archway, their boots scuffing the stone.

Then Calum said, "Walk with me."

I hesitated, brushing a stray lock of hair behind my ear. "Why?"

He glanced back at the guards, expression unreadable. "Standing still makes them nervous."

I rolled my eyes but stepped away from the railing. The terrace path led us through frost-bitten roses, their petals curled like ancient paper. My breath made small clouds in front of me as we walked under stone arches draped with ivy.

"You're very calm about all this," I ventured after a while.

He turned, tilting his head as though considering a puzzle. "All of what?"

I jabbed a finger between us. "Secret midnight meetings. Potential political nightmares. If my father discovers, he might try to kill you."

He considered that carefully. "I doubt he'd succeed."

"Not reassuring."

"Wasn't meant to be."

We came to a stop beneath an ancient oak whose bare branches laced a silver web against the sky. The trunk's bark was rough under my palm.

"You really don't take anything seriously, do you?" I asked.

He stared up at the twisting limbs, then back to me. "You think I don't?"

"You act like there are no consequences."

He drew in a breath so quiet I almost missed it. "Consequences always exist," he said softly.

I paused, the wind chafing at my dress.

"Then why behave like none of it matters?" I pushed.

He held my gaze, blue sparks dancing in his eyes. "Because once you pretend peace is permanent, you stop noticing the fractures."

I frowned. The branches overhead rattled in reply.

"What fractures?" I whispered.

He glanced up at the palace towers, their pinnacles etched in light. "Your father loathes my kind. My siblings distrust the fae. This treaty endures only because neither side believes it can win another war."

He turned back to me. "That isn't peace. It's exhaustion."

I bit my lip. "Bleak."

"Honest."

We resumed our walk, the path curling toward the edge of the gardens and the shadowed woods beyond.

"You're different than I expected," I said, tucking my cloak tighter around my shoulders.

"That ominous?"

"I was told you were cruel."

"I am."

"But also... observant."

He made a sour face. "That's not a compliment."

"And sometimes considerate."

"That definitely isn't."

My knees ached from leaning against the oak earlier. I glanced at him. "You defended that servant yesterday."

He shrugged, as if it were nothing. "Your father was bored."

"That's not the point."

"To him, it was."

We reached a small clearing where frost had painted every leaf silver. Calum stopped and looked at me with an intensity that made my pulse flutter.

"Why did you really invite me to the willow tree?" he asked.

"You already asked."

"And you didn't answer."

"I did."

"No." He was gentle but relentless. "You gave the diplomatic answer."

I pressed my back against the oak's rough bark, feeling its cool strength. Light filtered through the skeletal branches, scattering flecks of brightness across his hair.

"Maybe I prefer diplomacy," I said at last, my voice low.

"I doubt that."

"Why?"

His gaze never wavered. "You removed your crown before you met me."

I rolled my eyes. "You're obsessed."

"It was a choice."

"It was practical."

"It was rebellion."

I pressed my fingers into the bark. The echo of hushed

laughter, the distant ripple of fountain water, the soft sigh of the wind—they all felt like a promise and a warning at once.

"Tell me the real reason," he urged.

I stared past him at the palace spires, pulse throbbing in my throat. When I spoke, it was barely more than a breath. "Because you were the only person in that ballroom who didn't pretend to be someone else."

He went still. The clearing held its breath.

"And I wanted to know what that felt like."

He met my eyes, and for a heartbeat I saw something flicker there—something sharp, bright, and undeniably dangerous.

He whispered, "It feels dangerous."

I nodded, voice hushed but certain. "Yes. I think I'm starting to understand."

Under that ancient tree, in the thin winter light, we stood on the brink of something neither of us could fully name. And as the last leaf drifted down between us, I knew the real game had only just begun. And that Calum Ravenscroft, would be my downfall.

4

The palace feigned the serenity of slumber. Seelie castles, with their intricate magic woven into stone and timber, never truly yielded to stillness. Beneath the flagstones, I sensed it—a muted thrumming, an undercurrent that whispered through the soles of my slippers like an echo of my own heartbeat.

The muffled laughter of courtiers drifted faintly from the halls behind me, a woman's bright, effortless chime swallowed by the velvet curtain of night. Guards moved with diligent precision along their well-worn paths, each step a note in a rhythm I had memorized long ago—the thirty-second lull between the eastern terrace watch and the garden gate patrol.

Below, servants glided like shadows through the kitchens, and if I breathed deeply enough, I could still catch hints of the night's feast—honeyed wine, roasted quince, the sizzle of meat on searing iron.

But the gardens were claimed by the night.

Moonlight spilled over the winding paths, transforming statues and hedgerows into ghostly figures, their contours shifting with the breeze. A stone nymph I'd passed countless times now seemed alive, her outstretched hand glowing and accusatory. Night-blooming jasmine unfurled along the trellises, its heady scent clinging to the air so thickly it was almost intoxicating. Dew had already claimed the grass, darkening the hem of my gown as its silk whispered against my ankles.

I walked in solitude, and it was this solitude that was the issue. Each step away from the palace heightened the drumbeat of my pulse, a reminder that this was more than mere recklessness. My palms dampened with sweat, and I pressed them against the fabric at my sides, forcing my stride to remain steady, unhurried, as though simply savoring the evening air. As though my throat wasn't tight with the particular fear that accompanies deliberate defiance.

Should my father discover my tryst—a meeting with a god, no less—the consequences would be monumental, far beyond royal reprieve. I should have turned back. The safe path to my chambers beckoned, a tether pulling at my spine. Yet I pressed on.

At the garden's edge stood the willow, where the manicured palace grounds surrendered to the untamed forest. Even from afar, it was unmistakable—ancient, colossal, its trunk wider than three men side-by-side. Silver branches swayed in the midnight wind, producing a sound like silk being drawn across skin. Magic older than the castle, predating treaties and wars, infused it. Ever since childhood, I'd felt its presence—a pressure in the air, the taste of copper and rain, the feeling of unseen eyes. The grasses around its roots grew unruly, sheltering pale flowers that bloomed only in darkness. It was the perfect spot. No one watched. No one believed anyone would dare venture here.

As the clearing opened up, I slowed. The wind combed the willow's branches, revealing and concealing the space beneath in a rhythmic dance. The grass gave softly underfoot, its cool dampness creeping through my soaked slippers. Somewhere beyond, an owl's call echoed—two mournful notes before silence reclaimed the forest. The air felt charged, a crackle lifting the fine hairs on my arms.

For a brief moment, doubt crept in—perhaps he wouldn't come. Maybe he had toyed with me, retreating into whatever shadowed realm gods frequent when they tire of mortal games. Perhaps the encounter on the balcony had been nothing more than amusement, a transient curiosity. Relief and disappointment warred within me. Perhaps—

"You're late."

His voice, unmistakable, cut through the darkness like smoke, curling into every corner of the clearing before I could steady myself.

I halted. My breath snagged, held captive in my chest, as I fought to calm the sudden clamor of my pulse.

Calum emerged into the moonlight, his features stark in contrast. The light highlighted the planes of his cheekbones, the straight line of his nose, and plunged the rest into shadow —the hollows beneath his eyes, the firmness of his jaw, the line of his throat above the dark collar of his coat. He had shed the ballroom's finery for something simpler, darker, a garment that absorbed rather than reflected moonlight. He leaned against the willow as if its ancient power meant nothing, one shoulder to the bark, arms crossed, exuding an ease that defied the sanctity of the Seelie king's garden. The tree's magic pressed against my skin from a distance, but he stood within its embrace as casually as if leaning against a tavern wall.

"You're early," I replied, my voice steadier than expected— a small relief.

An eyebrow arched, a subtle movement that conveyed volumes. "That's your defense?"

"Observation," I countered.

A hint of a smile played at his lips—a suggestion rather than a full expression, gone almost as it appeared. "You look disappointed."

"I'm not."

"You didn't expect me to come."

"I thought you'd reconsider."

"And yet I'm here."

"Yes," I said. Here stood the God of Nightmares, beneath a willow in my father's domain as if he had every right, as if such trespasses were routine. A figure invoked by nursemaids to frighten children, his name whispered by courtiers only when necessary, now occupying the Seelie court without a hint of deference. The absurdity nearly undid me; a laugh threatened to bubble up, and I swallowed it.

"You're staring again," he said, the word *again* delivered with quiet precision.

"You're trespassing."

"A technicality."

"This is the Seelie court."

"And?"

"And you're not welcome."

Calum shifted from the tree, closing the space between us with deliberate ease. The willow's branches rustled in his wake, stirred by more than mere movement—a disturbance in the magic that reached my teeth. He stopped close enough for the night air to scent his coat, an earthy, mineral coldness beneath it, like stone after rain.

"Strange," he murmured. "You sounded very welcoming yesterday."

The moonlight filtered through the willow, casting restless shadows across the grass. The gardens were perilously quiet. The palace's distant laughter had faded, swallowed by the willow's ancient magic, or perhaps simply by distance. Even the owl had ceased its calls. We were alone.

"You didn't have to come," I said.

"No."

"Then why did you?"

He regarded me, as if measuring the scant space between us—the damp grass, the silvered light, the invisible border separating his world from mine. His eyes, dark in the dimness, held a flicker of curiosity, a calculation I couldn't quite decipher. Then, simply: "Curiosity."

"That's a dangerous reason."

"So is boredom."

I crossed my arms against the cold, the night deepening as I walked, the chill settling into my shoulders, my collarbones, where the gown exposed my skin. "You don't seem concerned about the consequences."

"You invited me," he pointed out.

"That doesn't mean I thought you'd accept."

"Why not?"

"Because you're supposed to be smarter than this."

His smile sharpened—a real one this time, altering the angles of his face, softening his jaw before adding a sharper edge to his eyes, making the base of my spine prickle with warning. "Princess, if I were smarter, I'd have left the ballroom before you followed me onto the balcony."

Something in my chest shifted, an irregular rhythm that owed nothing to fear and everything to how he said *Princess*— not as protocol, not as ceremony, but as a term he privately found amusing. "You assume I followed you."

"You did."

"And how would you know?"

He inclined his head, considering. The motion exposed the line of his throat, the shadow along his jaw, and momentarily caught the light on something at his collar—a chain, dark metal, disappearing into his shirt. "Because you're here."

His easy victory grated. My jaw clenched in frustration, and I felt my expression slipping, his amusement deepening as confirmation.

"If anyone hears of this," I warned, "the treaty could unravel."

"Yes."

"It could spark a war."

"That's not new."

"And yet you remain."

"Yes."

His calm was more unsettling than any threat. He delivered it without bravado, without any need to posture—just a flat acknowledgment, as if war were merely a matter of weather.

I scrutinized him, searching for signs—a twitch of dishonesty, the flutter of a pulse, the too-still hands of a liar. I found none. Either he was truthful or he was better at deceit than anyone I'd encountered. Both possibilities unnerved me equally. "Do you really not care what happens?"

"That depends."

"On what?"

His eyes met mine, unwavering. The wind stirred, bringing with it the jasmine's heavy perfume and the willow's green, ancient scent. "On whether this conversation is worth the trouble."

Willow leaves brushed my shoulder, cool and insistent, trailing across bare skin like fingertips. I flinched involuntarily.

Silence stretched—the kind that seemed tactile, thick with the sound of breathing, of inhalations held just shy of audible.

"And is it?" I asked.

Calum stood a pace away, shoulders squared, as if he could measure the night air with his gaze. Moonlight sifted through the willow's draping leaves, casting dappled shadows across his sharp features. He inhaled quietly, eyelids flickering, then let his stare travel over me inch by inch—lingering on my furrowed brow, tracing the high bridge of my nose, pausing where my lips pressed together, before snapping back to my eyes as though he'd found a clue there. Then he stepped forward on the soft grass, footsteps muffled, close enough that I could see the narrow white scar slicing through the dark stubble on his jaw, close enough, too, that the faint heat rolling off him felt like static against my skin.

"I haven't decided yet." His voice dropped low, each word poised on a knife-edge.

I crossed my arms, the silk of my gown whispering at my wrists. "You're insufferable."

A crooked smile tugged at one corner of his mouth. "I've been called worse."

A flicker of amusement lit his eyes, but he studied me again, gaze dipping to the empty sweep of hair above my ear.

"You took your crown off."

My fingers flew to my head. The silver circlet—its twin spirals of moonstone and opal—was gone. I'd left it behind, tangled in my braid by accident or by design.

"That was deliberate," he said, softer now, as though he could read my intention in the cool curl of my hair at my nape.

"It was practical," I lied.

"No. It wasn't." He glanced to the soft patch of grass where the circlet would have glittered. "That was when you decided you weren't coming here as the princess."

I said nothing. The willow's long branches stirred, brushing my cheek with a damp, earthy breath.

"And who did come?" he pressed.

The question hovered between us, heavy as the scent of night-blooming jasmine. I swallowed.

"A woman who is very tired of belonging to everyone else." My voice dropped to a hush.

His expression shifted—no pity, no condescension, but something sharper, a spark of recognition that made my heart bumble against my ribs.

"That," he said quietly, "I understand."

I felt the tight cage around my chest ease for the first time since I slipped beyond the palace gates.

We stood side by side in the willow's shadow: two strangers, two adversaries, two ticking disasters just waiting for a spark.

I lifted my chin. "Tell me something honestly."

He cocked his head. "That's dangerous."

"I know."

He hesitated, then nodded once. "Go on."

"Why did you come to the ball tonight?" I asked, voice threading through the rustling leaves.

He let out a low, amused breath. "To annoy your father."

I rolled my eyes, the fabric of my sleeve swishing against my hip. "I'm serious."

"So am I." His smile sharpened. "You think I risked crossing three realms just to irritate Oberon?"

I lifted one brow. "Yes."

"My siblings insisted diplomacy required my presence." He shrugged, the motion casual as if he wore centuries on his shoulders like a cloak. "And the treaty?"

I frowned, the word tasting bitter. "You don't believe in peace."

He turned so that lantern-dots from the distant palace glinted in his dark eyes. "I believe in pauses."

"Which isn't the same."

"No." He met my gaze, unabashed. "It isn't."

Silence fell again, punctuated by the tinny laughter drifting from the grand terrace and the shake of willow leaves overhead.

"You asked why I came," he said finally.

"So?" I prompted.

He studied my face as though searching for some hidden answer. Then he tilted his head. "Now I want to know something."

I braced myself.

"Why did you invite me here?"

My pulse thundered. In that glittering ballroom of courtiers and lies, he had been the only genuine thing I'd seen all night.

I lifted my chin, steady. "Because everyone in that palace fears you."

"That's common." His smile was patient, almost indulgent.

"And fear is lazy," I said. "I wanted to see if the stories were true."

He paused, as though tasting my words. Then he let his lips curve. "And?"

I met his gaze without flinching. "Some of them."

His smile blossomed, slow and deliberate. "That sounds promising."

I cocked my head back at him. "Don't get ahead of yourself."

"I rarely do."

I inhaled the damp earth, the faint tang of smoke from the torches. "You scaled the palace walls to meet the Seelie heir at midnight."

"That was your idea," he reminded me, amusement dancing in his eyes.

"And you followed it."

He shrugged. "Yes."

"Why?"

For the first time, Calum wavered, as if the question unsettled him more than any treaty.

Then, in a low murmur: "Because when you looked at me yesterday, Princess... you didn't look afraid."

The willow's leaves rustled overhead, a soft chorus to the moment's hush. I felt the space between us shrink, heat pooling at my temples. I stepped back, heart pounding.

"Careful," I warned.

His eyebrow rose. "Why?"

"Because if anyone finds out about this," I said, voice tight, "it will destroy more than a treaty."

He considered the quiet stretch of night, the distant palace lights like captive stars. "Perhaps."

Beneath the willow, we stood caught in that fragile pause —the first thread of something dangerous binding us together, silent and unseen. Neither of us noticed. Not yet.

The garden was not of the court. By that, I knew at once I should not have been there.

The paths were tighter, flagstones cracked and lifted by roots that no one had bothered to cut back. Moss grew in the seams, dark and damp, and where I stepped, the stone gave slightly underfoot, softened by years of rain and neglect. The hedges had been left to undulate in uneven, untamed arcs rather than the strict, geometric precision the Seelie demanded —they leaned across the path in places, close enough that their leaves caught the fabric of my sleeve as I passed, dragging lightly, releasing. The smell was different here. Not the cloying sweetness of the court's cultivated blooms, all honeysuckle and forced jasmine, but something earthier, greener. Wet bark. Cold soil turned by no hand. The faint, mineral tang of stone that had been damp for a very long time.

Overhead, the moonlight fractured itself through leaf and branch, casting silver bars across the ground, sharp amid the dark. The canopy was thick enough that the light came through in narrow, broken shafts, each one catching the tiny motes that drifted in the still air—pollen, perhaps, or dust from the crumbling walls. Where the light struck the ground, it was almost violent in its brightness. Where it didn't, the dark was absolute.

No lanterns, no servants, no one to bear witness. Only the hush itself—the kind of silence that has texture, that presses against the ears until the blood moving through your own veins becomes audible.

Breathing out, I let go of air like I was letting go of something secret, something that might otherwise be taken from me. The exhale left my lips warm and visible for half a second in the cool air before it vanished. My ribs loosened. The muscles across my shoulders, which I hadn't realized I'd been holding rigid since the last hall, since the last pair of watching eyes, released by slow degrees.

The farther in I walked, the lighter the pressure in the air became, as if the garden itself refused the oppressive gravity of the court just on the other side of the wall. I could still feel the wall's presence behind me—that high, smooth expanse of pale stone, lit from the other side by a thousand enchanted fires—but its influence thinned with each step, like wading out of deep water into the shallows. My breathing came easier. The tightness at the base of my skull, the one that lived there every hour I spent inside, began to dissolve.

That was what I wanted. Somewhere that did not look back at me.

I walked until the path curved and narrowed further, until the hedges rose above my head and the moonlight thinned to almost nothing. The ground here was softer—not mud, but something close, the flagstones giving way to packed earth scattered with fallen leaves. They were dry enough to crackle faintly underfoot, and I slowed my steps, conscious of the sound each one made in the heavy quiet.

A sound broke through—the silence shattering, but quietly. Not the scuff of shoes, nor the rustle of a body. Something finer, softer. Silk against stone, or the memory of it. A whisper of fabric so slight it could have been a leaf turning over in a breath of wind, except there was no wind. The air was perfectly, unnervingly still.

I stood very still.

My hand drifted to the place where my skirt gathered at my hip—not reaching for a weapon, because I had none, but for the comfort of something solid under my fingers. The fabric bunched in my grip. I held my breath. Counted the beats of my own pulse, thick and quick at the base of my throat.

"There you are."

His voice, from ahead, low and familiar enough that it pressed sharp below my ribs. Not a sound I heard so much as felt—the way certain notes on a low string travel through the chest before the ear registers them. It came from the darkness ahead, from a place where the moonlight didn't reach, and it carried no echo. The garden swallowed it whole.

My fingers loosened on my skirt. My pulse didn't slow.

Calum stepped from the thick shadow of an arbor, as if the darkness itself had given him shape, then reluctantly let him go. The arbor behind him was old, its wooden frame warped and furred with lichen, heavy with some climbing vine that had long since stopped flowering. He emerged from it the way smoke peels from a dying fire—gradual, the edges of him indistinct until he was fully in the fractured light.

He wore nothing of the court's shine tonight. Only a coat, dark and unfastened at the throat, sleeves shoved back so the bones and muscle of his forearms were exposed. The collar of his shirt beneath hung open, the linen creased, and I could see the hollow at the base of his throat, the skin there pale in the moonlight, the faint movement of his pulse visible just beneath the surface. The absence of any gold, any insignia, only made him look more real. More dangerous, for it. Without the armor of the court's finery, there was nothing to soften the sharp architecture of his face—the cut of his jaw, the deep-set eyes that caught what little light there was and held it without warmth. He looked like something the garden had grown on its own, something that belonged to the dark and the damp and the silence.

His hair was disordered, not artfully but carelessly, as though he'd dragged his hands through it more than once. A strand fell across his brow. He didn't push it back.

"You'll get yourself killed, wandering off like that," he said.

His voice was steady, unhurried. But his eyes moved—quick, practiced—over my shoulders, past me, checking the path behind me the way someone checks a perimeter. Making sure I was alone. Making sure no one had followed.

I tilted my chin. "Will I?"

"It's inevitable."

"You speak as though you'd be the one to do it."

He smiled, not with his mouth but somewhere behind his eyes, the curve so faint it could have been imagined. The muscles around his mouth didn't move. It was all in the gaze—a slight narrowing, a shift in the quality of his attention, the way a blade catches light when it turns. "If it were me, you wouldn't see me coming."

"I never do."

That made his gaze sharpen, as if something behind the surface of his face recognized me in some way. Not anger. Something more careful. His chin dipped a fraction of an inch, and the tendons in his neck drew taut, visible above the open collar. His hands, which had been loose at his sides, shifted—

the fingers of his right hand curling once, slowly, then straightening again. A gesture so controlled it could only be deliberate.

"You shouldn't be here," he said.

"And yet," I answered, moving a step closer, "you are."

The step brought me into the same shaft of moonlight that caught his shoulder, and I felt it on my face like cold water—bright and exposing. The earth beneath my foot was softer here, and my heel sank slightly. I didn't step back.

The silence between us grew. Not empty; not awkward. Just... expectant. Like a glass brimming but not yet spilling over. I could hear the faint, distant sound of the court beyond the wall—music, maybe, or just the collective hum of voices and enchantment—but it was thin and far away, belonging to a different world than this one. Here, the only sounds were breathing. His and mine. Slightly out of rhythm, neither of us willing to match the other.

I let my eyes drift past him, deeper into the garden's darkness. Beyond the arbor, the path continued into a kind of clearing—I could just make out the shapes of more hedges, a low stone bench draped in ivy, the skeletal silhouette of a tree that had lost half its branches. "Do you come here often?"

He shook his head. "No."

The word was flat. Final. He offered nothing more.

"Then why now?"

He looked at me for a moment without blinking, then turned away.

The movement was slow, deliberate—not an evasion but a direction. He turned his head first, then his shoulders followed, and the line of his body angled toward the deeper part of the garden, toward the clearing and the half-dead tree. His profile in the moonlight was severe. The shadows under his cheekbones were deep enough to hold water.

I followed the line of his gaze. At first, it seemed only a trick of the moonlight, or a shadow shifting in the trees. A flicker near the topmost branch of the skeletal tree, where the bark had gone white and smooth with age. Then it moved—a flick of black against the silvered air. Another. And another. Not birds. Too slow, too silent, too deliberate in the way they folded and unfolded against the night.

The air snagged in my throat and held.

Butterflies. Black as midnight, dozens of them, drifting like torn fragments of the night itself, their wings flashing iridescent when caught by stray light, then vanishing again into the dark. They moved without sound—no papery rustle, no hum of wing against air. They were utterly silent, which made them seem less like creatures and more like thoughts given form. Each one was slightly different in size, in the cant of its wings, but they all shared that same quality of being not wholly real, nor wholly imagined. Something between. Their edges blurred when I looked at them directly, sharpened when I caught them from the corner of my eye. The iridescence, when it came, was not a color I could name—something between deep violet and oil-black, shifting, alive for a half-second before the wing turned and swallowed itself back into shadow.

They drifted among the bare branches, along the tops of the hedges, through the still air of the clearing. One passed close enough that I felt the displacement of air against my cheek—or thought I did. It might have been nothing.

Without thinking, I stepped forward. My foot found a dry leaf, and the crack of it seemed enormous in the quiet.

"They're beautiful," I breathed.

The word left me on almost no air at all, barely voiced, and I watched one of the butterflies spiral slowly downward, tracing a helix in the dark, before rising again on some invisible current.

"They're nothing," Calum said.

His voice had changed. Flatter. Stripped of the wry edge he'd carried a moment before. He stood with his arms at his sides, and I noticed that his hands were very still—too still, the kind of stillness that takes effort. The tendons on the backs of his hands stood out like fine cords.

I stopped. "You made them."

It was not a question.

He looked away, jaw tight. The muscle at the hinge of his jaw bunched and released, bunched again. A vein traced a line down the side of his neck, and I watched it pulse—once, twice—steady but quick. "Just shadow. It doesn't cost anything."

"That isn't true."

His eyes snapped back to mine. The movement was fast enough that a strand of hair fell across his brow again, and this time he did push it back—an impatient, almost rough gesture, his fingers raking through it and leaving it worse than before.

I didn't look away. "You don't do anything without a price," I said.

He didn't answer at first. His mouth pressed into a thin line, and I watched him swallow—the slow bob of his throat, the way his chin lifted almost imperceptibly afterward, as if bracing against something.

All around us, the butterflies shifted, falling lower, brushing my arms, my hair. Their touch was cool, more like the chill of a thought than a living thing—not the dry, papery brush of real wings but something finer, something that left a trace of cold on the skin the way breath leaves fog on glass. Faint and fading. One landed on my wrist, wings opening and closing, patient and slow. I could see through it, almost. The moonlight on my skin showed through the dark membrane of its wing, and where it rested, the tiny hairs on my arm rose. Not from fear. From the sheer strangeness of it—the weight that was not quite weight, the life that was not quite life.

Alive. Or nearly.

"Why butterflies?" I asked.

His face changed. Not blank, but guarded. Closed. The openness that had been there—barely there, the width of a crack in a door—shut. His brow smoothed. His mouth lost its tension. The transformation was precise and practiced, and I recognized it because I'd seen it a hundred times across the court: the face he wore when someone asked a question he hadn't prepared for. The difference was that here, in the dark, with no one else watching, the mask looked like what it was. A mask. And the effort of putting it on was visible in the slight flare of his nostrils, the way his chest rose and held before he let himself breathe again.

I watched him measure the question, and then weigh the risk of an answer. His eyes moved—not away from me but across me, reading something in my expression the way you'd read a document for traps.

"I don't know," he said, at last.

"You do," I said quietly.

He set his jaw. "I said I don't know."

The words came harder this time, each one placed like a stone in a wall. His shoulders had drawn up, just slightly—a fraction of an inch, but enough to change the line of his body from easy to braced.

I stepped closer. Close enough to feel the heat of him radiate, the space between us thinning, every line of tension drawn tight. Close enough to smell him—not perfume, not the court's cloying incense, but something simpler. The warmth of skin. The faint, clean bitterness of whatever soap he used, nearly gone by this hour. Beneath it, something darker, harder to name. Like the air before a storm, metallic and charged.

"You know," I said.

He watched my hand, the way it hovered by his sleeve. His

gaze tracked it with the focus of someone watching a flame brought near paper. The muscles in his forearm twitched—I could see them, laid bare where his sleeves were shoved back, the fine dark hair there catching the light—but he didn't pull away. Didn't move at all.

Then, with careful deliberation, he reached out—not for me, but for one of the butterflies. His hand moved slowly, fingers extended, and the nearest one drifted toward him as if drawn. It folded up as he caught it, dissolving into nothing, leaving a shimmer in the air like a fading memory. The shimmer lingered for a moment, a faint distortion in the dark, and then that too was gone. His fingers closed on empty air. He held them there, curled, before letting them fall.

"I only make them when I want something to stay," he said.

The words hit, heavy and soft as dark velvet. They landed somewhere in my chest and settled there, warm and aching, and I felt my own breath change—felt it stutter and catch before I could control it.

Something inside me shifted. Not gently. Like a key turning in a lock that had rusted shut, the mechanism grinding, the bolt giving way with a sound you feel in your teeth.

I stared at where the butterfly had been. The air there was still faintly cooler than the rest, as if the shadow had left a residue. "Stay?"

His mouth twisted, not quite a smile. Sharper than that. The kind of expression that lives in the space between bitterness and acceptance, that knows exactly what it's admitting to and hates itself for the admission.

"They don't," he said.

"Then why make them?"

He met my eyes this time, and there was no mask left. Only a dangerous kind of truth. The kind he never allowed when others could see. His pupils were wide in the low light, the dark of them nearly swallowing the pale ring of color around them, and there was something raw in the way he held my gaze—unflinching, but not steady. The way someone holds still when they know that moving will make the wound worse.

"Because I can pretend they will."

The breath left me, slow and unsteady. I felt it go—felt the air leave my lungs in a thin, shaking stream, felt my chest hollow out and my throat tighten around what remained.

The butterflies pressed closer, a tide gathering in the space between us, drawn by him, or by what he could not say. They orbited slowly, wings barely moving, and the air around us grew cooler with their presence, the chill of them accumulating until I could feel it on my bare skin—my arms, my collarbones, the strip of exposed neck above my dress.

One brushed my cheek, so light it could have been imagined. A whisper of cold that traced the line of my cheekbone and was gone.

"Show me," I said.

He frowned. "Show you what?"

"How you do it."

"I did."

"No," I said, closing the last of the distance. My skirt brushed his boot. I could feel the warmth of him now, not just radiating but pressing—close enough that the air between us had its own temperature, its own weight. "Show me properly."

His pupils widened. I watched it happen—the black expanding, slow and involuntary, swallowing the thin ring of grey-green around it until his eyes were almost entirely dark. His breath came in through his nose, controlled, but I saw the effort in it—the way his nostrils flared, the way the tendons in his neck drew taut.

"That's a mistake."

"Why?"

"Because you'll want more."

"And?"

"I don't give things twice."

I let a smile, small and sharp, cross my lips. "Then I'll value it."

That was enough.

A crack, thin as a hairline fracture, split his composure. I saw it happen in real time—the way his expression broke along a fault line he hadn't known was there. His brow creased. His lips parted, just barely, and I heard the soft click of his mouth opening, the start of a word he didn't say. His hand, the one that had caught the butterfly, opened at his side, fingers spreading, and I saw the faintest tremor run through them before he caught it and held still.

He lifted his hand.

The air shifted, as if the world held its breath. I felt it in my ears first—a change in pressure, subtle, like the moment before thunder when everything goes flat and close. The temperature dropped by a degree, then two. The moonlight seemed to thin, as if something was drawing the light itself toward a single point.

Shadows stirred at the edges of everything, pulling toward him, toward us, gathering from every hollow and crease. I watched them move—watched the darkness under the hedges deepen and stretch, watched the shadow pooling beneath the stone bench reach out a long, thin arm toward where he stood. The dark at the base of the dead tree shifted and flowed like water finding a new channel. All of it moving toward his hand, toward the space between his fingers, as if he were the drain at the center of the night.

"Don't move," he said.

His voice was lower now, rougher, as if the effort of what

he was doing had stripped something from it. His eyes were fixed on his own hand, and in the moonlight I could see a fine sheen of sweat at his temple, just at the hairline, catching the silver light.

"I wasn't going to."

"Good."

The first butterfly formed between his fingers, shadow folding inward, shaping along lines finer than silk. I watched it happen from inches away—watched the darkness compress and gather, thickening from translucent to opaque, the edges sharpening like a blade being honed. Wings first, impossibly thin, the veins of them visible as slightly darker lines within the dark. Then the body—slender, segmented, precise. Each antennae drawn out of darkness as if it had always belonged to him, curling forward with a delicacy that made my throat ache. The whole process took no more than a few seconds, but I felt each one. The air between his fingers was colder than the rest, cold enough that when I breathed, I could taste it—something sharp and clean, like the first breath after snow.

It fluttered once, twice, and rose. The movement was so real—the slight wobble of a new thing finding its balance, the uneven first wingbeats—that I had to remind myself it was shadow. Just shadow. But the cold trace it left on my skin as it passed my face was real enough.

Another came after. And another. They spun up, not just from his hand, but from the night itself, as if his making of the first had given the darkness permission. They emerged from the deep shade under the arbor, from the pooled black at the base of the hedges, from the crevices in the crumbling wall. Each one pulled itself into being with the same precise, shivering compression—a fold of shadow, a sharpening, and then wings. Until the space around us was filled with their slow, spiraling storm.

I laughed, soft and surprised. The sound left me before I could catch it, startled out of me by the sheer impossible density of them—hundreds now, maybe more, their wings overlapping and layering until the air itself seemed to be made of moving dark. They caught the moonlight in flashes, each iridescent flicker brief and brilliant, like sparks struck from flint, and the effect was dizzying. A galaxy of cold, dark wings, turning and turning around us in a helix that rose from the ground to the bare branches overhead.

"They listen to you."

He shook his head. "No. They don't."

But even as he said it, the butterflies nearest to him shifted their orbit, adjusting their path as his hand moved, tracking the slight gesture of his fingers the way iron filings track a magnet. He either didn't notice or chose not to.

A butterfly landed on my shoulder, another on my palm, a third against my throat. Each point of contact was a small, precise shock of cold—not unpleasant, but vivid, the way the first touch of metal against bare skin is vivid. The one on my palm opened its wings fully, and I could feel the faint pressure of each wing against my fingers, lighter than paper, lighter than breath. The one at my throat rested just above my pulse, and I wondered if it could feel the beat of it through whatever substance it was made of.

"They do," I insisted.

He watched each place the shadows touched. His gaze moved from my shoulder to my palm to my throat, and at each point it lingered—not casually, but with an intensity that had weight, that I could feel as surely as the butterflies themselves. His lips had parted slightly, and I could see the edge of his teeth, the lower lip bitten faintly white where he'd pressed it.

"They're just fragments of me," he said, the words nearly a whisper. His voice had gone hoarse, scraped thin, and the admission seemed to cost him something physical. I watched his shoulders drop a fraction, as if a wire holding him upright had been cut.

"And fragments of you listen," I said.

Something flickered in his face, gone before it could be caught. A contraction of the muscles around his eyes—not a wince, not a flinch, but something close to both. The ghost of an expression that might, in someone less guarded, have been grief.

He looked away. "Careful. You're starting to sound like you believe that."

"I do."

That startled him. I saw it. The way his eyes widened, how his breath caught and stuttered before he forced it steady again. His chest hitched—a visible, involuntary jerk—and his hand, the one that had been shaping the butterflies, dropped to his side and curled into a fist. Not in anger. In the way you grip something when the ground shifts under you.

"You shouldn't," he said.

"Why not?"

"Because you're wrong."

I tipped my head. "Am I?"

"Yes."

"Prove it."

The silence was thicker now, almost physical. Even the butterflies held still, as if the garden itself wanted to hear. Their wings stopped mid-beat, hundreds of them suspended in the air around us, and the sudden absence of their movement made the quiet deeper, denser, a living thing pressing in from every side. I could hear Calum breathing now—not steady, not even. Short, controlled pulls of air through his nose, the kind of breathing that takes concentration. The kind you use when your body wants to do something your mind won't allow.

"Tell them to leave," I said.

His jaw set. The muscle at the hinge bunched hard enough that I could see the shape of it under his skin. "They don't take orders."

"You said they're pieces of you."

"They are."

"Then make them leave."

A pause. A long one. His eyes searched my face, moving back and forth between my eyes as if the answer to something was written there in a language he was still learning to read. A butterfly drifted between us, slow and silent, and neither of us moved to brush it aside.

"They won't," he said, low. The word came out rough, almost scraped.

"Or you won't?"

His eyes flashed. A hard, bright flare of something—not anger, or not only anger—that lit his gaze from behind and made the pale ring of color around his pupils momentarily vivid. "It isn't the same."

"It is," I said.

The butterflies didn't move. They pressed closer, if anything. The cold of them accumulated on my skin, a dozen points of chill that I felt individually now—on my arms, my wrists, the exposed line of my collarbone. The air between us was dense with their dark wings, and through them I could see his face in fragments, in glimpses between their slow, hovering bodies.

One grazed my lip. The cold of it was startling there, sharp and intimate, and I felt my mouth open slightly in response, an involuntary parting, the breath I drew tasting of shadow—of something clean and lightless and very, very old.

Another tangled in my hair. I felt it working itself into the strands, its wings catching and folding, and I didn't reach up to free it.

"They like you," I said.

He was sharp, almost angry: "No. They don't like anything."

His voice had risen, just slightly—not in volume but in pitch, the careful control of it fraying at the edges. His hands were both fists now, the knuckles pale, and I could see the rapid beat of his pulse in the hollow of his throat, quick and visible.

A deliberate smile, slow as shadow. "Then why are they staying?"

That reached him; I saw it in the way his whole body tightened, the way his hand curled as though holding back from something—or someone. His spine straightened. His chin dropped. The breath he took was audible—a sharp, short intake through his teeth—and his eyes went very bright and very dark at the same time, the pupils blown wide but the gaze behind them blazing.

"They'll disappear," he said.

"When?"

"Soon."

"And if they don't?"

"They will."

"And if they didn't," I said, even softer, not quite touching him, my fingers hovering so close to his sleeve that I could feel the warmth of his arm through the fabric, the fine hairs on my own hand rising toward him as if magnetized, "would you keep them?"

His gaze dropped, tracing the line of my mouth, my throat, the pulse beating steady there. I felt his attention on each place like a physical thing—like fingertips that never quite made contact, hovering just above the skin, close enough to feel the heat of. His breathing had gone shallow. I could see the rise and fall of his chest, quick and tight, the fabric of his shirt moving with each breath.

"I don't keep things," he said.

"That isn't true."

His eyes snapped up. The look in them was stripped bare—no mask, no guard, no carefully constructed blankness. Just the raw, exposed nerve of someone who has been seen in a place they thought was hidden. His lips pressed together and then parted, and I watched him try to find the mask and fail. Try again and fail again. His throat worked—a hard, visible swallow—and a muscle in his cheek twitched, once.

"You don't know what you're saying."

"I know you made these," I said, my hand sweeping lightly through the butterflies. They parted around my fingers like smoke, their cold trailing across my skin, and reformed in my wake. "And I know it's because you wanted something to stay."

He didn't answer. Not at once. His jaw worked silently, and I watched him fight with something—some word, some admission that was trying to surface and being pushed back down. His eyes were glassy in the moonlight, too bright, and he blinked once, hard, as if to clear them.

Then:

"Careful, Ottilie."

My name in his mouth. Low, rough, the syllables given weight they didn't normally carry. He said it the way you'd say a word in a language you'd learned late in life—carefully, with full awareness of what it meant, each sound deliberate and placed.

"Why?"

"You'll start expecting things from me I won't give."

I didn't look away. "Then don't give them to anyone else."

There. That was it. The change.

Small, invisible to anyone but me.

But I felt it—the shift in the air, how he went so still even the night seemed to hesitate. The butterflies around us slowed, their wings dropping to half-speed, as if the force that animated them had faltered. His face didn't change. His body didn't move. But something behind his eyes collapsed—some final wall, some last defense—and what was left was so open, so unguarded, that looking at it felt like looking at a wound. His mouth softened. The lines of tension around his eyes released. And for one breath, maybe two, he looked exactly like what he was: someone who had been alone for a very long time and had just been told he didn't have to be.

"Don't do that," he said.

"Do what?"

"Make it sound simple."

"It is simple."

"It isn't."

"It is, to me."

His voice dropped, a threat and a promise both: "What happens when simple things stop being enough?"

I didn't waver. The butterflies on my skin held still, their cool weight steady, and I met his gaze through the dark veil of their wings. "Then we make them enough."

The butterflies moved again, not away but inward, crowding every inch between us until there was nothing left but that soft storm of wings and the hush at its heart. They filled the space so completely that I could barely see him through them—only fragments, only glimpses. The line of his jaw. The hollow of his throat. One eye, dark and unblinking. The cold was everywhere now, all around me, a cocoon of shadow and chill, and at its center, the warmth of him. The two sensations layered against each other—cold and warm, dark and close—until I couldn't tell where one ended and the other began.

He looked at me as if I'd said something dangerous.

As if I'd said something true.

The silence held. One heartbeat. Two. Three. I counted them in the pulse at my throat, each one heavy and distinct, and I watched him stand inside the moment like someone standing at the edge of a very high place, deciding.

"Then don't leave me anywhere I can't follow," he said.

Not loud, but it struck harder than anything before. The words came out rough and low, barely more than breath, and they broke somewhere in the middle—not dramatically, not obviously, but in the slight catch between *can't* and *follow*, the tiny fracture in his voice that he couldn't smooth over in time. His eyes held mine, and they were wet. Not crying. Not that. But the brightness in them was not the moonlight.

I couldn't breathe, for a moment.

Not out of fear.

But because I understood. The weight of what he'd said, the cost of it, settled over me like something physical—like the butterflies themselves, landing one by one on every part of me until I was covered in the cold, dark proof of what he'd made. What he'd made because he wanted something to stay. And here he was, asking me to be that thing. Not in those words. He would never use those words. But in the only language he had —in shadow, in the careful, trembling architecture of creatures made from darkness and wanting—he had said it plainly.

"I won't," I said.

My voice was steady. I made it steady. I owed him that.

And for the first time, he believed me.

I saw it in the way his shoulders dropped—not in defeat but in release, the way a held breath finally leaves the body. In the way his fists uncurled, fingers spreading slowly, trembling faintly at the tips. In the way the butterflies around us surged once, all at once, a single pulse of dark wings that lifted and fell like a shared breath, and then settled again into their slow, spiraling orbit. Calmer now. Steadier.

He didn't smile. He didn't reach for me.

But the space between us changed. Became something that held, rather than divided.

And the butterflies stayed.

6

Secrets burgeon like poisonous blooms in a place such as this—tendrils twisting into hidden corners before you even know they're there. You learn that truth when you're young, if you're meant to survive: every hushed syllable slipping from pale lips, every swift flicker of an eye under gilt masks, every sudden absence that can't be smoothed over—the Seelie court gathers it all, storing each scrap until the web is so tight no secret can slip free. Curiosity here is as vital as breath; without it, the court would wither like a flower deprived of sun.

So the longer I met Calum Ravenscroft in the midnight gardens, the more certain I grew that our furtive footsteps would be trailed, our stolen words exposed.

For a while, though, the court's eyes were fixed elsewhere.

The gods had descended in gilded carriages, their laughter echoing through marble halls as ambassadors from distant fae realms streamed behind them. Every corridor became a silent arena for political sparring—velvet-robed advisors whispering over treaties, their words ricocheting off stone columns. Delegates volleyed ancient grievances like jeering hawks. All attention was riveted on the dance of diplomacy.

None were watching me.

Not closely enough, at least.

Publicly, Calum and I did not speak. That unwritten decree emerged swiftly—and it saved us more than once. By day, beneath chandeliers of crystal droplets, we passed each other like strangers. He lingered by his siblings—the God of Nightmares, regal and carved of shadows. I perched beside my father, the dutiful heir, every breath measured to mirror Oberon's mood.

But after dusk, the gardens unfurled their secret realms for us alone.

I discovered hiding places deeper than I could have dreamed. A great weeping willow by a moonlit pond, its silver tendrils draping like silk curtains. A secluded glade beyond marble fountains, where white moonflowers cradled dewdrops even in frost. A narrow track skirting the forest's edge where lantern glow faded, and moss carpeted the ground. And once, half-swallowed by ivy, a crumbling shrine whose ancient stones murmured with residual magic.

Always, whenever I slipped through the iron gates, Calum stood waiting—still as a dark statue, yet alive with expectation.

In those first nights, we argued more than we spoke. He unraveled my every comforting illusion about the court, the treaty, the fragile peace that bound gods and fae.

"You keep calling it peace," he said once beneath the silvered boughs, where the wind whispered through leaves.

"That's exactly what it is," I replied, voice tight.

He shook his head, tossing a stray lock of midnight hair from his brow. "No. It's a pause."

I crossed my arms. "You're very fond of that theory."

"I've watched this cycle repeat."

"What cycle?"

"Peace built on suspicion."

"And?"

"It never endures."

I paused on the mossy path, the scent of damp earth rising around us. "You really think there's another war looming?"

"Not yet," Calum admitted, his tone as gentle as twilight.

"That's comforting."

He fixed me with eyes that reflected starlight. "But inevitable."

His certainty burned brighter than any threat.

Still, I returned each night.

Maybe because he challenged me instead of feigning interest, as everyone else did. Maybe because he saw beyond the crown to the girl beneath. Maybe because the danger was intoxicating.

Rumors took root two weeks later like frost cracking the pond's surface.

I sensed them first in the soft hush that fell when I entered a chamber—the sudden lilt of voices lowered, glances grazing my back too long. Subtle shifts, but in the Seelie court, suspicion was a sharper weapon than any accusation.

That realization crystallized during an evening council.

My father presided at a long marble table in a grand hall carved with swirling vines. Advisor voices tumbled over one another in heated debate over border rights and ancient debts, their echoes colliding with gilded pillars. I sat at his side, nodding when required but letting their words wash over me like distant rain.

On the far dais, the gods lingered—silent, inscrutable.

Alistair murmured counsel into one ear of a trembling courtier. Nora, silver hair gleaming like molten moonlight, held still as sculpted ivory. Calum watched from a tall window, slumped in boredom. He never met my gaze here.

Nora did.

Her pale eyes glinted as they found mine, her smile a knife's edge. Then she turned her head toward my father.

"Your daughter seems restless tonight," she said, voice as smooth as creamed honey.

The chamber fell into a charged hush. My father's gaze slid to me. "Ottilie appreciates the gravity of these talks," he intoned evenly.

"Oh, I do not doubt it," Nora replied, her tone thawing into casual warmth. "I simply wondered if the court has been... sufficiently entertaining."

A delicate taunt, but it landed heavily. My father's jaw tightened. "My daughter has most ample duties."

"Of course," Nora murmured, as though she covered nothing at all.

Yet for an instant, her eyes flicked toward Calum, his silhouette dark against the starlit glass.

My heart stuttered cold.

Calum gave no sign. If he noticed, he hid it beneath that mask of indifference.

Nora's lips curved into a faint, dismissive laugh. "Forgive me. I find diplomacy so riveting that I forget we all harbor smaller intrigues."

The council resumed its clamor, but I felt the threads tighten around me.

When the session broke, I slipped away, heart thrumming in the marble-clad corridors lined with alabaster statues. Shadows pooled in alcoves as courtiers drifted apart. I was nearly at the wide staircase when a soft voice stopped me.

"You look troubled."

I turned to find Nora close beside me, her presence sharp

and luminous. Candles flickered along the walls, casting her pallid face into shifting light and shadow.

"You startled me," I whispered.

"Forgive my intrusion." Her smile sharpened. "You seemed... preoccupied."

"I was reflecting on the council's matters."

Her silver eyebrows rose. "I highly doubt that."

She stepped nearer, her perfume of winter jasmine drifting between us. "I believe you've been pondering my brother."

The words sliced through the hush.

"I don't know what you mean," I said, swallowing.

"Oh, Ottilie." She sighed, a sound like wind through dead leaves. "This palace is hardly vast."

I forced calm into my voice. "You're making assumptions."

"Am I?" Her pale stare pinned me. "You vanish each evening. My brother vanishes each evening. Coincidence wears thin."

The corridor walls seemed to inch closer, torchlight guttering.

"You misunderstand," I insisted.

"Perhaps," she conceded, "or perhaps I see far more than most."

"And what is that?"

Her lips curved in a mocking half-smile. "Someone clever enough to hide something dangerous."

Then she brushed past, her skirts whispering against the flagstones. Before the shadows swallowed her, she added softly, "Be careful. Calum Ravenscroft is... skilled at leaving ruin in his wake."

Then she melted into darkness.

I remained frozen, heart pounding like a drum.

That night, I hesitated by the glowing lanterns that lined the inner courtyard. I lingered until their golden light pooled into nothing, until the palace sighed with quiet. But my feet led me inevitably to the gardens.

Calum awaited me beneath the willow, its pale leaves twinkling like stars.

"You're late," he said, voice drifting with the rustle of branches.

"I had… company."

"Your sister."

I met his gaze. "You know?"

"Of course." He pushed away from the willow trunk, the bark rough beneath his fingertips. "She confronted you."

"Yes."

"And?"

"She believes we are hiding something."

A small, mirthless smile curved his lips. "We are."

"That's hardly helpful."

He studied the ripples on the moonlit pond. "You're afraid."

"I am not."

"Then why do your hands shake?"

I looked down. My fingers trembled against the soft grass as a night breeze rose, carrying whispers of distant laughter.

"Nora warned me about you," I confessed, voice low.

Calum's smile flickered, sharp as broken glass. "Isn't that rich?"

"Why?"

"She's the last person who should issue warnings."

I swallowed. "What do you mean?"

He stepped closer, silhouette framed by the glowing moon-flowers. "She said I leave destruction behind me."

"Yes."

"Did she mention who usually strikes the spark?"

His bitterness was a deeper cut than any threat. I opened my mouth to answer but found no words.

He watched the trembling edges of my reflection in the water. Moonlight glinted off his eyes—cold and relentless.

"I could stop meeting you," I blurted.

Silence rippled between us.

"Could you?" he asked softly, each word drifting like a leaf on still water.

I hesitated, my heart threatening to betray me.

He studied my face, then allowed a slow, certain smile to unfold.

"That's what I thought."

After Nora's warning, I told myself the meetings would end. That was the sensible decision, the one expected from a princess raised to measure the precise weight of peace between gods and fae. The responsible choice. The only choice, if one believed in the brittle arithmetic of power.

Instead, I found myself returning to the willow tree the next night.

The path from my chambers wound through the eastern colonnade, where the marble had been worn smooth by centuries of careful footsteps. I kept to the shadows between the pillars, bare fingers trailing along stone so cold it burned. The guards changed rotation at the quarter-hour—I'd counted the intervals weeks ago, mapped the gaps in their patrol routes like charting stars. Through the postern gate, across the flag-stone terrace where ice had begun to web the cracks between the stones, and then down the sloping lawn where the grass grew long and silver in the dark. The willow stood alone at the garden's far edge, its curtain of branches sweeping the ground in slow, pendular arcs, as if the tree itself kept time with some rhythm older than the court.

Calum was already waiting. He always was.

At first, I had thought it a matter of chance: sometimes I arrived early, sometimes late, but always, he was there, waiting beneath the arching silver branches, his presence as inevitable as the moon's rise. Eventually, the pattern unsettled me. Whether the moon was bright or just a pale knife above the horizon, Calum stood in the clearing, as if he'd divined the exact moment I would arrive. I'd tested it once—left an hour earlier than usual, taking a different route through the servants' passage behind the kitchens, where the air still smelled of woodsmoke and rendered fat. He'd been leaning against the trunk, arms crossed, head tilted back as though he'd been watching the branches sway for hours. Not a trace of surprise when I parted the curtain of leaves. Just that steady, unhurried attention, like a compass needle finding north.

Tonight, I pushed through the willow's veil—the thin whip-ends of the branches catching against my cloak, dragging lightly across my jaw—and found him standing exactly where I expected, one shoulder braced against the trunk, the silver bark pressing a faint pattern into the dark fabric of his coat.

"You're early tonight," he said when I stepped into the open.

"You say that every time."

"And I'm right every time."

His voice carried the particular weight of someone stating fact rather than opinion. The corner of his mouth moved—not quite a smile, more the suggestion of one held in reserve.

Moonlight threaded through the willow, catching the faintest frost where it clung to the grass. Each blade held its own thin casing of ice, and when the wind stirred, the frost crackled in tiny, crystalline whispers, almost inaudible beneath the deeper sound of the branches swaying. An illusion of gentleness, if one looked only at the surface. Beneath the frost, the ground was hard as iron, and the roots of the willow pushed up through the earth in gnarled ridges that caught at my boots.

"You didn't answer my question yesterday," I said.

"Which one?" He moved with precise economy, as if nothing ever surprised him. A slight shift of weight from one foot to the other, a repositioning of his hands—from crossed arms to one hand loose at his side, the other still resting against the bark. Each movement deliberate, calibrated. Like a swordsman between exchanges.

"The one about Nora."

Calum leaned against the tree. "That's because you didn't ask a question," he said. "You accused me of avoiding one."

The distinction landed with the precision of a needle. His eyes—pale, the color hard to name in the dark, somewhere between grey and something colder—held mine without wavering.

I folded my arms; a childish gesture, but necessary. The posture put distance between us, or at least the illusion of it. My fingers dug into the wool of my sleeves. "Fine. Then I'll ask it properly."

He waited, still and expectant. The silence between us filled with the sound of the wind moving through the willow's canopy, a low, continuous hush, like water running over stones far away.

"What did you mean when you said she lights the match?"

His amusement vanished. The shift was immediate—a tightening along his jaw, a subtle flattening of expression, as though a door had closed behind his eyes. For a moment, his attention slipped past me, toward the cold glow of the palace windows. From here, they looked like distant hearths, warm and golden, but I knew the light came from enchanted sconces that gave off no heat at all.

"My sister," he said at last, "has always believed the world is easier to control when people are taught to fear the wrong things."

His voice had changed register—lower, more careful, each word placed with the deliberation of someone laying stones across a river.

I frowned. The muscles between my brows tightened, and I felt the expression settle into my face like something familiar. "I don't understand."

"That's intentional."

The answer grated. It scraped against something raw in my chest—the particular frustration of standing at the edge of understanding and being denied the final step.

"You're doing it again."

"Doing what?"

"Speaking in riddles."

"Not riddles," he said with a dismissive flicker. His hand moved—a brief, cutting gesture, fingers spreading and then closing, as if brushing away something trivial. "Observations."

I stepped closer, pushed by impatience. The frost crunched beneath my boots, and the sound was louder than I expected in the clearing's hush. Close enough now to see the faint lines at the corners of his eyes, the way the moonlight carved the planes of his face into something sharper than daylight ever revealed. "If Nora believes our meetings are dangerous, perhaps she's right."

"Of course she's right."

I blinked, caught off guard. The admission sat strangely in the air between us, like a blade offered handle-first. "That was quick."

"You're the Seelie heir," he said. "I'm the god most likely to start a war."

"That's a rumor."

"That's a statistic."

I tried not to smile at the sharpness of it. My lips pressed together, fighting the pull. Something warm flickered behind my ribs despite the cold.

"You're comfortable with the reputation."

"It saves time."

"And yet you keep meeting me."

His gaze sharpened. The pale eyes narrowed a fraction, and his chin lifted—a minute adjustment, but it changed the geometry of his attention entirely, focusing it to a point. "Yes."

"Why?"

For a heartbeat, no answer. The wind died. The willow branches stilled, hanging motionless around us like the ribs of some vast, sleeping creature. He moved away from the tree, slow and thoughtful, as if measuring the perimeter of our silence. His boots left dark impressions in the frosted grass, and I watched each print fill slowly with the returning white.

I followed, willow branches brushing against our shoulders, their touch a reminder of the boundaries we crossed. The thin ends were ice-slicked, and they left cold trails of moisture on my cloak, soaking through to the skin beneath.

"You asked me once why I came to the ball," he said.

"Yes."

"I told you it was to annoy your father."

"You implied there was more."

"There always is," he said.

We left the clearing behind, the narrow path leading us toward the hush of the forest. The ground changed beneath our feet—from frost-brittle grass to packed earth and fallen leaves, their edges curled and brown, crackling with each step.

The air thickened with the smell of damp bark and cold soil and something deeper, older—the mineral scent of stone and root and centuries of undisturbed growth. Behind us, the palace lights seemed to recede, swallowed by distance, shrinking to pinpricks between the dark trunks of ash and oak.

"Do you know what gods hate most?" he asked.

"What?"

"Predictability."

"That seems unlikely."

"It's true."

"Why?"

"Because it means someone else has already written the story."

He stopped so abruptly I nearly collided with him. My hand shot out instinctively, catching at his sleeve, and for an instant I felt the fabric of his coat beneath my fingers—fine-woven, colder than it should have been, and beneath it, the hard line of his forearm, the faintest vibration of something that was not warmth but something adjacent to it, something that hummed at a frequency my bones recognized before my mind did.

I released him. Stepped back. My palm tingled.

"And tonight," he said, very quietly, "I'm doing something very predictable."

"What's that?"

"Meeting a princess I absolutely should avoid."

The honesty left me raw, stripped to the bone. The words settled into me the way cold water fills a glass—all at once, without warning, taking the exact shape of the space they'd been poured into. My throat tightened. I swallowed against it.

"You could stop," I said.

"Yes."

"But you don't."

"No."

I looked up at him. "Why?"

The question was heavier this time, as if the air itself demanded an answer. The forest had gone silent around us—no wind, no rustling, no distant call of night birds. Only the sound of my own breathing and the faint, rhythmic pulse I could feel in my wrists and throat.

Calum's gaze moved across my face, slow and deliberate, as if memorizing something he fully expected to lose. His eyes tracked from my forehead to my jaw, pausing at my mouth, then rising to meet my eyes again. The muscles in his throat shifted as he swallowed.

"Because when I'm with you, I forget how much I hate this world."

The words stunned me. I could not find breath. My lungs locked. The forest tilted—just slightly, just enough that I had to widen my stance to keep my balance—and then righted itself, leaving me standing in the aftermath of something I hadn't been prepared for.

"You shouldn't say things like that."

"Why not?"

"Because they sound sincere."

"They are."

I laughed, a thin thread unraveling in the dark. The sound was wrong—too high, too brittle, the kind of laugh that lives closer to its opposite. "That's worse."

"Why?"

"Because sincerity is reckless."

"I'm aware."

We stood in silence, with only the wind threading through the forest, carrying the scent of winter pine—resinous and sharp, the smell of sap frozen mid-bleed—a quiet warning. Above us, the canopy shifted, and a sliver of moonlight fell between the branches, painting a narrow stripe of silver across the ground between our feet.

"You're trembling," Calum said.

"I'm cold."

"No, you're not."

I looked down. My hands betrayed me, shaking. Not the fine tremor of cold—I knew that tremor intimately, had felt it through hundreds of winter councils and dawn patrols along the northern border. This was different. This came from somewhere deeper, somewhere behind my sternum, a vibration that radiated outward through my arms and into my fingers, which would not stay still no matter how hard I pressed them against my sides.

"Your court is watching you," he said, voice low. "Your sister is suspicious. Your father already hates my existence."

"Yes."

"And yet you're still here."

"Yes."

"Why?"

The echo of my own question, turned back on me.

I considered lying. The words were there, readily available —duty, curiosity, strategy, all the acceptable reasons a princess might meet with a foreign power under cover of night. The silence between us demanded more. The silence had teeth.

"Because when I'm with you... I feel like myself."

The truth slipped out, unguarded. It tasted like blood— warm, copper-bright, the flavor of something that should have stayed inside.

Calum went very still. Not the careful stillness of before— not deliberate, not controlled. This was the stillness of something struck. His shoulders locked. His breath caught, a barely audible hitch, and his hands, which had been loose at his sides, curled slowly into fists and then released. The knuckles whitened, then flushed.

"That's a dangerous thing to admit."

"I know."

"You could lose everything."

"I already belong to everything."

The wind shifted. It came from the north now, carrying with it the distant sound of the palace bells marking the hour—a single, low tone that resonated through the trees and faded into the earth. We stood suspended in that moment, neither willing to retreat. The space between us had its own gravity, its own weather.

Calum stepped closer, close enough that I could feel the hum of power in his skin, the gravity of his presence bending the air. It was a physical sensation—not warmth exactly, but pressure, the way the atmosphere thickens before a storm. The hairs on my arms rose. My skin prickled with awareness, each nerve ending pulling toward him like iron filings toward a lodestone.

"You're very brave," he said softly.

"No," I whispered. "I'm very foolish."

"Those are often the same thing."

My pulse was loud, thunderous in my ears. I could feel it in my temples, in the hollow of my throat, in the tips of my fingers. A war drum, steady and relentless.

"You should go," I said.

"I should."

"Before someone notices you're missing."

"Someone already has."

That stopped me. The words landed like a stone dropped into still water, and I felt the ripples move through me—chest, stomach, spine.

"Who?"

"Alistair."

My stomach twisted. A cold knot, sudden and tight, pulling everything inward. "He knows?"

"He suspects."

"That's not better."

"No."

"Is he angry?"

Calum's shrug was almost apologetic. One shoulder lifted, held, then dropped—a gesture stripped of its usual ease, weighted with something he wasn't saying. "He's concerned."

"That sounds worse."

"It usually is."

I hesitated. My teeth found the inside of my cheek, pressing hard enough to taste the faintest copper. "Then maybe this really should stop."

Calum didn't move. Instead, he reached for me, brushing a loose strand of hair from my face—a gesture so gentle it left me unsteady. His fingertips grazed my temple, traced the curve of my ear, and tucked the strand behind it. The touch lasted perhaps two seconds. It burned a line across my skin that I would feel for hours afterward, a phantom warmth that no amount of cold could erase.

"You don't want it to stop," he murmured.

"No," I admitted.

His hand lingered, then dropped. His fingers curled at his side, as though holding the ghost of the contact.

"That makes two of us."

The distance between us was gone. I could feel the warmth radiating off him, the subtle shimmer of divinity threading through his breath. It moved like heat haze—visible if I looked at him from the corner of my eye, invisible when I looked directly. A distortion in the air, a bending of the light, as though the world around him was not quite solid enough to contain what he was.

"This ends badly," I whispered.

"Yes."

"We both know that."

"Yes."

"And you're still standing here."

"Yes."

Something inside my chest tightened, sharp as a blade. Not pain—or not only pain. Something fiercer, something with edges that cut in both directions.

I met his eyes. He watched me the way someone watches a storm beginning to coil itself in the sky—not with fear, exactly, but with the absolute attention of a person who understands that what comes next will change the landscape.

"You should walk away," he said.

"Why?"

"Because if you don't..."

He left the sentence unfinished. The silence it left behind was louder than any word.

"Because if I don't what?"

He lowered his voice, barely more than a breath. I felt it against my skin—warm, close, carrying the faintest trace of winter air.

"I won't."

The world narrowed: the forest, the moonlight, the wind through the willow—all of it falling away. The sounds dimmed. The cold receded. There was only the space between us, contracting with each heartbeat, and the look in his eyes— unguarded, undefended, stripped of every careful layer he wore like armor.

"You're very confident," I said.

"No. I'm very certain."

My heart pounded, reckless. I could feel it in my whole body now—not just in my chest but in my throat, my wrists, the soles of my feet against the frozen earth.

"This is the moment," he said, "when sensible people leave."

"And if I'm not sensible?"

"Then this is the moment everything changes."

We stood locked in that precipice. The air between us hummed—taut as a bowstring, vibrating with potential energy. One breath. Two. I could see the pulse in his throat, steady and quick.

I stepped forward.

And kissed him.

The contact was abrupt, electric, irrevocable.

His lips were colder than I expected—cool at the surface, then warm beneath, like river water in autumn. The taste of him was sharp and clean, like winter air at altitude, like frost on metal. My hand found the front of his coat, fingers twisting into the fabric, anchoring myself against the vertigo that swept through me.

For a moment, he didn't move. His body was rigid, suspended between impulse and control, and I felt the tension in him like a held breath, like a drawn bow at full extension. Then his hand closed around the back of my neck—firm, certain, his fingers threading into my hair—and the kiss deepened, the world tilting sharply beneath us.

His other hand found my waist, steadying me, or steadying himself—I couldn't tell which. The hum of power in his skin intensified, buzzing against my palms through the layers of fabric, and the air around us thickened with a pressure that made my ears ring. Somewhere far away, a branch cracked under the weight of ice, the sound sharp as a snapped bone.

Moonlight spun across the clearing.

And somewhere inside me, something terrible took shape: this was the moment—the precise, faultless instant—when everything began to fall apart.

The first kiss should have been an ending.

Sensible stories would have demanded it: one mistake beneath a willow, a lapse followed by swift return to order. But sensible stories do not last long in royal courts. And they never survive around gods.

The night after our kiss, I told myself not to go back. I paced my chambers until the candles guttered in their sconces, wax pooling on the silver trays, the smell of tallow thick and cloying. I sat at my desk and opened correspondence I had no intention of reading, the parchment rough under my fingertips, the ink blurring as my focus slid away. I pressed my hand against my mouth and felt the ghost of him there—the pressure, the cold-then-warmth, the way his breath had mingled with mine.

I lasted until midnight.

The clock in the corridor struck twelve—deep, resonant chimes that vibrated through the stone walls and into the soles of my feet. Before the final note had faded, I was reaching for my cloak.

Cold wind moved the willow branches as I entered the clearing once more. The frost had thickened since the previous night, and the grass crackled like crushed glass beneath my boots. The willow's canopy was heavier with ice, the branches drooping lower, their tips glazed and glittering. When I pushed through them, ice fragments scattered against my shoulders and melted in cold rivulets down my neck.

Calum was waiting.

He stood in the same place—shoulder against the trunk, arms loosely crossed—but something in his posture had changed. A looseness in his stance, an ease that hadn't been there before, as though some internal mechanism had been released. The moonlight caught the line of his jaw, the hollow beneath his cheekbone, the faint curve at the corner of his mouth.

He didn't speak at first, only watched as I approached, the faint curl of a smile at his mouth, as if he already knew the outcome of this night. His eyes tracked my progress across the clearing with an attention that was neither casual nor intense —simply present, simply certain.

"You're late," he said.

"You say that every time."

"And I'm right every time."

I stopped a few paces away. Close enough to see the frost that had gathered on the shoulders of his coat, the thin crystals catching light like scattered salt. Close enough to feel the edge of that hum—that constant, low-frequency vibration of divinity that surrounded him like heat from a banked fire.

"You're very certain of that."

"You keep proving me right."

His amusement was quiet, but it kindled something reckless in me. A spark behind my sternum, bright and dangerous.

"You're impossible," I said.

"And yet you kissed me."

The memory stole the air from my lungs. I felt it again— the shock of contact, the cold-warm pressure of his mouth, the way his hand had closed around the back of my neck with a certainty that left no room for doubt. My lips parted. I pressed them shut.

"You're remarkably direct about that."

"I prefer honesty."

"That's a dangerous preference in this court."

"That's why I rarely visit."

I folded my arms, searching for a shield. The wool of my

cloak was rough against my wrists, and I gripped it harder than necessary, my nails digging small crescents into the fabric. "We shouldn't have done that."

"No," he agreed. His expression didn't change—no regret, no defensiveness. Just that steady, level regard, like someone acknowledging the weather.

"That's not the response I expected."

"You expected me to argue."

"I expected you to justify it."

"Why would I?"

"Because it was reckless."

"It was," he said. "And you're still here."

"Yes."

The simplicity of the exchange unsettled me. Each response stripped away another layer of pretense until what remained was bare and unadorned: two people standing in a frozen garden, choosing to be exactly where they shouldn't be.

Wind sifted through the willow leaves, a sound like distant voices—murmuring, conspiratorial, as though the tree itself was keeping a record of our meetings.

"We need rules," I said.

Calum's eyebrow arched. A single, precise movement—the left brow rising while the right stayed fixed, an expression that managed to convey skepticism, amusement, and challenge in equal measure. "Rules."

"Yes."

"That sounds suspiciously like responsibility."

"Which we clearly need."

He considered this. His head tilted slightly, and his gaze drifted upward, following the line of a branch where ice had formed in delicate, fern-like patterns against the bark. "Very well. What rules would you like, Princess?"

The title sounded different now, sharpened by memory.

Before, it had been a formality—a word he used the way one uses a key, to open a particular door. Now it carried the weight of the previous night, of his hand in my hair, of the way he'd said nothing at all when we finally pulled apart, only looked at me with an expression I still couldn't name.

"First," I said, "we do not speak during court."

"Already happening."

"Second, we only meet in the gardens."

"That limits the scenery."

"Third, this ends if anyone discovers it."

He tilted his head, as if weighing the claim. The movement was slow, deliberate, and his eyes narrowed a fraction—not in suspicion but in assessment, the way a card player studies a hand that's been played too quickly.

"Does it?"

"Yes."

"That sounds optimistic."

"Why?"

"Because your court already suspects something."

My chest tightened. The knot was back—cold, dense, pulling at the space beneath my ribs.

"Who?"

"Everyone with eyes."

"That's not helpful."

"It's accurate."

I looked back at the palace, its towers lit by lanterns like stars caught in glass. The light spilled from a hundred windows, warm and golden against the dark stone, and I could see the silhouettes of figures moving behind the curtains—servants, advisors, guards. Each one a potential witness. Each one a thread that, if pulled, could unravel everything.

"Your sister already confronted me," I said.

"Yes."

"And my father watches everything."

"Yes."

"And yet you're still here."

"Yes."

"You're infuriating."

"That's what you said yesterday."

"And the day before."

"And the day before that."

I let the breath out slowly. It clouded in the air between us, a pale ghost that dissolved almost immediately.

"This cannot last."

"Nothing does."

"That's not comforting."

"It's honest."

He stepped closer, the air around him shifting, the pressure of his divinity subtle but unmistakable. I felt it against my skin like the change in atmosphere before rainfall—a heaviness, a charge, the sense of something vast moving just beyond the edge of perception. The frost on the grass nearest to him had thinned, I noticed—not melted, exactly, but softened, as though his proximity altered the temperature of the air in ways that had nothing to do with heat.

"You're afraid," he said.

"I'm cautious."

"You're afraid."

"Yes," I admitted. The word tasted like iron in my mouth.

"Good."

"That's not reassuring."

"It means you understand the stakes."

He glanced back at the palace, its windows burning against the night. The light caught the angles of his face and threw the rest into shadow, and for an instant, he looked less like a man and more like what he was—something ancient, something vast, wearing a shape that was convenient but not quite truthful.

"Your court is changing," he said.

"What do you mean?"

"The advisors whisper more than they used to."

"Courts always whisper."

"These whispers feel sharper."

I frowned. The familiar tightening between my brows, the familiar weight of a concern I couldn't yet name. "You've only been here a few weeks."

"That's long enough."

He looked at me, direct. His eyes caught the moonlight and held it—not reflecting, exactly, but containing it, the way deep water contains light, pulling it inward rather than sending it back.

"Something is shifting beneath the surface of this treaty."

"You're imagining things."

"No," he said. "I'm recognizing patterns."

"What patterns?"

"The kind that lead to war."

The word hung between us, heavy. It pressed against the air like a stone dropped into snow—no sound, only the slow, spreading impression of weight.

"There will not be another war," I said.

"Why not?"

"Because no one wants one."

Calum's smile was thin, stripped of humor. His lips barely moved—a tightening more than a curve, the kind of expression that lives in the muscles around the eyes rather than the mouth.

"Wars rarely begin because people want them."

"Then why do they begin?"

"Because someone decides they're inevitable."

The wind lifted, cold and certain. It cut through the garden with a sound like tearing silk, carrying with it the scent of frozen earth and something sharper—smoke, perhaps, from a distant chimney, or the acrid tang of enchantment worked too close to iron.

I didn't like the way he said it. The words had the quality of something rehearsed—not because they were false, but because they had been true so many times before.

"You're very determined to believe the worst."

"I'm very experienced."

We walked, slow and measured, through the garden's labyrinth of hedges and fountains, the palace lights faint through the trees. The hedges rose above our heads, their leaves dark and dense, frosted at the tips like sugared confections. The fountains had been shut off for winter, their basins filled with ice that had frozen in layers—clear at the bottom, cloudy white at the surface, the trapped air forming small, ghostly bubbles. Our footsteps echoed against the flagstone paths, and the sound bounced off the hedge walls and returned to us slightly altered, slightly delayed, as though the garden were repeating our movements back to us with a half-second lag.

"I spoke with Alistair today," Calum said.

"That sounds ominous."

"It was."

"What did he say?"

"That my presence makes everyone nervous."

"That seems obvious."

"He's worried about you."

My steps faltered. My boot caught on an uneven stone, and I stumbled—barely, just a hitch in my stride—but enough that Calum noticed. His hand moved toward me, instinctive, then withdrew before it made contact.

"Why?"

"Because he's not blind."

"That's not reassuring."

"He also thinks this court is playing a deeper game."

I frowned. "What game?"

"He didn't say."

"Then how do you know?"

"Because my brother never warns me unless it matters."

Silence settled along the path. It was a different silence than the one beneath the willow—denser, more watchful. The hedges pressed in on either side, and the shadows between their branches seemed to thicken, as though the garden itself were listening.

Something about the conversation left me uneasy. A sensation at the base of my spine—not quite fear, not quite recognition. The feeling of a door opening in a room I thought was sealed.

"You're imagining conspiracies," I said.

"Perhaps."

"But courts do not risk war lightly."

"Courts don't," Calum said. "But individuals do."

We reached the edge of the gardens, where the trees grew dense and the world narrowed to shadow. The ornamental hedges gave way to older growth—oaks with trunks as wide as doorways, their bark fissured and black with age, and beneath them, the undergrowth tangled in frozen brambles that caught at the hem of my cloak. The air was colder here, the kind of cold that settles into the lungs and stays.

"Your father hates me," Calum said suddenly.

"That's not exactly a secret."

"He hated me before we met."

"Many people do."

"I didn't give him many reasons."

"That's debatable."

Calum laughed quietly. The sound was low and brief, more breath than voice, and it made something shift behind his eyes—a momentary softening, quickly corrected. "Fair."

Wind moved through the branches. The oaks creaked—deep, arthritic sounds, the protest of old wood forced to bend. Somewhere above us, an owl called, its voice sharp and solitary in the dark.

"You should go back," he said.

"Why?"

"Because if you stay much longer, you'll miss the evening council."

I glanced toward the palace, where lanterns had flared brighter. The windows of the great hall blazed—someone had lit the chandelier, its enchanted flames throwing patterns of gold and amber across the snow-covered courtyard. Figures were moving inside, their shadows long and distorted against the curtains.

"Are you coming?"

"To the council?"

"Yes."

"Gods rarely attend meetings about paperwork."

"That's reassuring."

"Is it?"

"Yes. Because if you were in that room, my father would start a war before the first document was signed."

Calum grinned. It was the most unguarded expression I'd seen from him—wide enough to show teeth, quick enough to feel stolen. "Now that sounds entertaining."

"You're terrible."

"I've been told."

I hesitated, then stepped closer. The frost crunched between us, and the distance shrank to something intimate—

close enough to see the faint shadows beneath his eyes, the way the cold had drawn color into the sharp line of his cheekbones, the almost imperceptible tension in his jaw.

"You're certain something is wrong," I said.

"Yes."

"And you don't know what."

"No."

"That's comforting."

"It shouldn't be."

I studied him, searching for reassurance and finding only more questions. His face gave nothing away—or rather, it gave away exactly what he chose, and what he chose tonight was a careful, measured blankness that was itself a kind of answer.

"Then why are you still here?"

Calum looked at the palace, then back at me. The light from the great hall caught his profile—the strong nose, the set of his mouth, the line of his throat where a muscle tightened and released.

"Because," he said softly, "whatever game your court is playing..."

His eyes met mine, steady as moonrise. The pale irises held the reflected light of the palace windows, twin points of gold against grey.

"I don't think you're the one pulling the strings."

The wind moved again, rattling through the trees. The oaks groaned. Ice cracked somewhere in the darkness, a sharp, splitting sound like a bone breaking under pressure.

And somewhere in the heart of the Seelie palace, someone was already beginning to pull them.

8

Time passed, but not in the way the court measured it. Not in treaties, nor in seasons, nor even in the thin red lines of wars. Time passed in stolen nights. In the hush of hidden corridors where the torches had been allowed to gutter low, in the brush of knuckles against knuckles when we passed each other in crowded rooms, in the slow, perilous loosening of something I had once vowed to never let take hold. Love.

The doors opened.

They were enormous things—oak darkened with age and banded in iron that had gone green at the rivets—and they groaned inward on hinges that hadn't been oiled in decades, as though the cathedral itself were reluctant to let this happen. Light flooded through the gap, pale and slanting, thick with dust motes that turned gold as they drifted. Incense hung in the air, clove and myrrh and something older beneath it, the mineral smell of stone that had been standing for centuries. Candles lined the nave in their hundreds, their flames bending in unison as the draft from the open doors reached them.

For a moment, the world shrank to a single, burning point: him.

Calum Ravenscroft waited at the altar, a statue cast in shadow and refusal, dressed in ceremonial black that seemed to sharpen every edge of him—the hard line of his jaw, the ridge of his collarbones where the high collar opened just enough to show the base of his throat. The court had tried; I could see the effort in the careful tailoring, the silver thread worked into his cuffs, the polished buttons meant to catch the candlelight and make him gleam like something tamed. The attempt to make him seem ceremonial, less of a threat. They had failed. His shoulders filled the coat like something caged inside it, the fabric pulling taut across his back when he shifted. His dark hair had been combed but was already falling forward, one strand cutting across his brow like a crack in marble. He looked as though he had been forced into the room, into their customs, but would never be theirs.

Still, he stood and waited. His hands were at his sides, fingers loose but not relaxed—the difference was subtle, the kind of stillness that came from discipline rather than ease.

The whispers began at once, trailing after me down the aisle, cold and persistent as ghosts. Silk rustled against pews. Fans snapped open to hide moving mouths, though they did nothing to muffle the sound. *This is a mistake. This will end in blood. He will ruin her.* The words slithered between the columns, echoed off the vaulted ceiling, multiplied.

I heard every word. I ignored every one.

Because Calum wasn't looking at them. His gaze had found me the instant the doors opened and hadn't moved since—dark eyes fixed on mine with an intensity that made the candlelight feel cold by comparison. He saw only me.

And in that gaze, I found what I had learned to name: not

gentleness, nor safety, but certainty. The kind that sat in the chest like a second heartbeat, steady and immovable.

"Stand straight," my father muttered at my side. His hand was a weight on my arm, his fingers pressing into the crook of my elbow hard enough that I could feel each one through the layers of lace. His jaw was set, the muscle in his cheek twitching the way it did when he was swallowing something he wanted to say in front of the wrong people.

I kept my eyes ahead. "I am."

"This is not a performance."

"No," I said, voice low. "It isn't."

Because it wasn't politics. It wasn't strategy. It wasn't peace. It was a choice, and I had already made it.

The aisle stretched before me, cathedral vast and echoing, the stone floor worn smooth by centuries of processions, pale grey veined with darker grey like a map of old rivers. Every step was a public reckoning, each footfall landing with a muted click that the acoustics caught and amplified, so that the entire nave could hear the rhythm of my approach. The pews on either side were packed —lords and ladies in silks the color of bruises and deep water, their faces arranged in careful, studied neutrality that fooled no one. I could feel their eyes like the prick of needles along my arms, my neck, the bare skin above my bodice. The bouquet in my hands —dark roses, nearly black at the center, opening to a deep, bruised red at the edges—trembled once. I tightened my grip until the stems bit into my palms through the ribbon wrapping.

Closer. Closer. Closer.

The incense grew thicker near the altar, sweet enough to coat the back of my throat. The candle flames steadied. The whispering thinned, then died, as though the congregation had collectively run out of air.

Until I stood before him.

This close, I could see the details the court couldn't—the faint scar that disappeared into his hairline above his left temple, the almost imperceptible tension in the cords of his neck, the way his chest rose and fell just slightly faster than it should. He smelled of cedar and something sharper beneath it, like the air before a storm.

"You're late," Calum said, voice pitched just for me. His lips barely moved.

A huff of laughter escaped, quiet enough that only he could hear it, warm against the cool air between us. "I was walking down the aisle."

"You took your time."

"You're insufferable."

"And yet here you are."

A flicker of amusement crossed his face—the slightest twitch at the corner of his mouth, a fraction of a degree's lift in one dark brow. Brief, gone before anyone else could see it. But I did. I always did.

My father released my arm. The absence of his grip left a dull ache where his fingers had been, and I resisted the urge to rub the spot. He stepped back, and I heard rather than saw him take his seat—the creak of the pew, the sharp exhale through his nose.

The priest started speaking. His voice was reedy and practiced, rolling through the old words with the kind of careful reverence that came from repetition rather than belief, the syllables bouncing off the high stone ceiling and returning as echoes of themselves. I didn't listen, not really. Because Calum's hand found mine—and the moment our fingers laced together, his skin warm and rough-callused against my own, the world seemed to steady. The whispers, the watching, the weight of every expectation pressing down on us from every direction—all of it receded to a low hum, like a sound heard through water.

"This is your last chance," he said quietly. His thumb rested against the inside of my wrist, and I knew he could feel my pulse hammering there, quick and defiant. "To run."

I stilled. My fingers tightened around his. "And leave you standing here?"

"I would survive."

"No," I said, just as soft. "You wouldn't."

His hold tightened. The calluses on his palm scraped against my skin, and I could feel the slight tremor in his grip—barely there, the kind of thing you'd miss if you weren't looking for it. "You don't understand what you're choosing."

"I do."

"There will be war."

"There already is."

"They'll turn against you."

"They already have."

A pause. The shift of breath between us—his exhale, my inhale, the air passing warm and close in the narrow space that separated us. A candle somewhere to our left guttered and spat, sending a brief tendril of smoke curling between us before it dissolved.

He dropped his voice. "I will not be gentle, Ottilie."

"I don't want gentle."

His eyes searched mine, sharp and dangerous—the pupils blown wide in the low light, the dark irises ringed with something almost amber at the edges—and something almost afraid. A tightening around his eyes, the faintest pull at the skin between his brows, as though something behind his expression was bracing for impact. That was what undid me. Not the monster the court feared. Not the god they whispered about. But the man in front of me, jaw set and hands unsteady, giving me one last chance to turn away.

"Then stop me," I said.

A long silence, stretched thin as thread. The candles flickered. The congregation held its breath—or perhaps that was only me.

He didn't move, didn't let go, didn't turn away. "I won't," he said. The words landed low and final, like a stone dropped into deep water.

"I know."

The vows were next. The priest gestured with a liverspotted hand, and the cathedral seemed to lean inward, the shadows between the columns deepening as though the building itself was listening. This, at least, I felt. Every word. Every syllable settling into my bones like something being carved there.

"I, Calum Ravenscroft, take you, Ottilie Valentine..." His voice altered, lower, heavier, stripped of the sardonic edge I knew so well. Every word rang with truth, resonating in the space between us and in the hollow of my chest. His grip on my hands shifted, and he held them the way you hold something you're afraid of breaking—firmly, but with a careful awareness of every point of contact.

His thumb brushed my pulse. A slow, deliberate stroke across the thin skin of my wrist, as though he were counting the beats.

"You are the moon to my endless night," he said, and the words struck something deep—a place behind my ribs that I hadn't known was waiting to be named. Not because they were crafted to impress, not because they were the kind of thing poets carved into marble, but because they were unembellished and true. His voice caught on the word *moon*, barely, a roughness like cloth snagging on a nail.

"The only thing in this world I would burn it down to keep."

A ripple of unrest moved through the court—a collective intake of breath, the creak of bodies shifting in pews, a fan snapping shut somewhere in the third row like a small, sharp rebuke—but I did not look. I looked only at him. At the way the candlelight caught the edge of his jaw, the way his throat worked when he swallowed.

"I vow that no matter what comes..." His voice dropped, almost a promise in the dark, spoken into the space between his mouth and mine. "...I will always choose you."

My throat tightened. Not with fear, not with doubt. Something worse, fragile, breakable—a glass thing balanced on a ledge, trembling with each gust of wind. Something I could lose. My eyes burned, and I blinked hard, once, because I would not cry in front of these people. Not here. Not where they could use it.

"I, Ottilie Valentine, take you, Calum Ravenscroft..." My voice came softer than I meant, the words catching on the incense-thick air, but steady. I held his gaze and didn't let go. "To be my anchor in a world that was never meant to hold us."

His fingers tightened their grip—a reflexive clench, knuckles whitening, as though the words had landed somewhere physical.

"You are the shadow that keeps me safe," I told him. I smiled, small—barely a curve of my lips, but enough that the skin around my eyes creased, enough that he could see it even if no one else could. "And the fire that reminds me I'm alive."

The room, the court, my father—all of it faded. The rows of watching faces blurred into a wash of silk and candlelight. The stone columns became shadows. The priest became a voice without a body. There was only Calum, and the warmth of his hands around mine, and the sound of my own heart in my ears.

"I vow to stand beside you when the world turns against us." Because it would. I could already feel it—the pressure building like weather on the horizon, dark and inevitable. "I vow to love you without restraint..." I drew breath, tasting incense and cedar and the faintly metallic tang of something I couldn't name, and chose. "...until the stars burn out."

My gaze did not waver from his. "And long after."

"I do," he said. His voice was rough at the edges, scraped raw, and his eyes were bright in a way that had nothing to do with the candlelight.

"I do," I answered.

The magic sealed it. Not violently, not cruel—no flash of light, no crack of thunder, nothing so dramatic. But with gravity. With permanence. I felt it settle over us like the weight of deep water, pressing against my skin, sinking into the marrow of my bones. Something old and implacable wound around us, invisible but undeniable, tightening like roots growing through stone, binding us in a way no court could undo. The candle flames flared—all of them, simultaneously, stretching tall and blue-white at their tips—and then settled back to gold. The air tasted different. Heavier. Charged, the way it feels after lightning has struck close.

And then he kissed me.

Not careful, not restrained, not the polite, closed-mouth press the court would have preferred—the kind of kiss you could paint and hang in a gallery, bloodless and appropriate. Reckless. Possessive. Alive. His hand came up to the side of my face, fingers sliding into my hair and scattering pins that hit the stone floor in tiny, bright sounds like rain on a window. His other arm wrapped around my waist and pulled me flush against him, and I could feel his heartbeat through the layers of black wool and white lace, hammering in counterpoint to mine. He kissed me like it was an argument he intended to win, and I let him, and I kissed him back with the same ferocity, my fingers curling into the lapels of his coat.

The court gasped, a hush like a breaking wave—a single, collective sound that rolled through the nave and crashed against the far wall. Somewhere, a chair scraped. Somewhere, my father made a sound I chose not to interpret. I didn't care. I kissed him back. If the world was going to end, I wanted this moment first.

When we broke apart, I was laughing. The sound bubbled up from somewhere deep and unguarded, too loud for the cathedral, too bright for the solemnity the court demanded. I couldn't stop. His forehead rested against mine, and I could feel his breath on my lips, fast and warm.

"Think we scandalized them enough?" I whispered.

"Not even close," Calum replied, hand tight on mine, his thumb pressing into the center of my palm. "We've got time."

We ran. Out of the cathedral, past the priest who stood with his mouth still open mid-benediction, past the pews where lords and ladies sat frozen in various states of outrage and disbelief, past the iron-banded doors that were still standing open, spilling us out into the blinding afternoon. The sun hit my face like a slap, warm and golden after the incense-dim interior, and I squinted against it, laughing still, my free hand gathering fistfuls of my skirt so I wouldn't trip on the cathedral steps. The stone was warm under my thin-soled shoes. Away from the watching eyes, away from the brittle order the court pretended to hold—I could hear shouts behind us, voices calling my name, my title, but the wind snatched them apart and scattered the syllables. I didn't think, didn't question. I ran with him.

"Calum!" I called, out of breath and giddy, the word half-swallowed by the wind that whipped my veil back behind me like a banner. "Where are we going?"

"You'll see."

"That's not reassuring."

"You love it."

I did. Gods, I did.

The city blurred past—cobblestones slick with the morning's rain, the smell of wet stone and bread from the bakeries on the lower terraces, the startled faces of merchants and flower sellers who pressed themselves against their stalls as we flew by, a bride in white and a groom in black running like fugitives through streets that had been hung with bunting they hadn't asked for. Calum's grip on my hand was iron, unyielding, pulling me around corners and down narrow lanes where the buildings leaned close enough to block the sky. My lungs burned. My legs ached. I had never felt so awake. The world fell away in layers—first the noise, then the buildings, then the cobblestones giving way to packed earth and then to soft ground that yielded under our feet—until there was only forest, only the two of us, only the sound of our breathing and the crunch of leaves and the distant, vanishing hum of the city behind us.

When we stopped, it felt like stepping into another world. A clearing opened before us, ringed by birch trees whose bark peeled in white scrolls, their canopy filtering the light into shafts that fell like pillars of hammered gold. Water spilled over a shelf of dark stone—not a waterfall, not quite, but a steady curtain of it, catching the light and shattering it into fragments that danced across the moss-covered rocks below. The pool at its base was clear enough to show the pebbled bottom, greens and silvers and greys, and the water moved with a gentle, constant murmur that filled the silence without breaking it. Ferns grew thick along the edges, their fronds curled at the tips, and the air smelled of wet earth and something sweet—wild honeysuckle, maybe, or the sap bleeding from a broken branch somewhere nearby. Untouched. The kind of place that felt as though it had been waiting.

"It's beautiful," I breathed. My chest was heaving, and a strand of hair had come loose from its pins and was plastered to my damp forehead.

"Not as beautiful as you."

I rolled my eyes, hard enough that he could see it. "You didn't even hesitate."

"I never do."

"That's concerning."

"You married me anyway."

"Regretting it already."

"You're lying."

I smiled. The kind that crept up slowly and settled in, warming my face from the inside. "I am."

"I love you," I told him, because I needed to. Because something in me, slow and deep, like a tide pulling back from shore, felt as if it was running out of time. The words came out quieter than I intended, half-lost in the sound of the water, and I watched them land on his face—the way his expression shifted, opened, became for one unguarded second something raw and undefended.

He pulled me into the water, his arm hooking around my waist and tipping us both off the mossy bank. The cold hit me like a wall—shocking the breath from my lungs, turning every nerve to a bright, singing wire. I shrieked, the sound ringing off the rocks, then laughed, the two sounds tangling together in my throat. I clung to him, fingers digging into the soaked wool of his shoulders, and felt the water soak through my dress in seconds, the heavy fabric dragging at my legs, my hair coming fully loose and spreading across the surface in dark, floating ribbons. Alive, unbearably alive—every inch of skin prickling with cold and warmth where his body pressed against mine.

"You've ruined my dress," I gasped. Water dripped from my eyelashes, blurring him into streaks of black and gold. The lace was already going translucent, clinging to my arms like a second skin.

"What a tragedy." His voice dropped, heat threading through it like a current beneath the cold water, his lips close enough to my ear that his breath raised goosebumps along my neck. "Guess we'll have to fix that."

"Calum—"

"We should—"

I stopped. Looked at him. Really looked. The water had darkened his hair to ink, slicked it back from his face so there was nothing to hide behind—no shadows, no sharp angles of composure. Just him. The scar at his temple. The line of his mouth, softened now, almost uncertain. The rise and fall of his chest, quick and uneven. Water beaded on his skin, catching the fractured light.

"Do you want to stop?" he asked. His voice was quiet. Careful in a way he almost never was, the vowels held gently, as though the question itself was something fragile he was placing in my hands.

And there it was again. The moment, the choice, the chance to walk away. He gave it every time. Every time, he opened the door and stood aside and waited to see if I would walk through it or turn back.

I bit my lip, tasting cold water and the faintest trace of the dark roses from my bouquet where I'd pressed my face to them earlier. Then smiled—slow, deliberate, the kind of smile that was itself an answer. "Hell no."

His mouth found mine, and the cold water didn't matter anymore.

And for a small, fragile while, the world let us have this. The light through the birch canopy shifted as the sun moved, painting us in slow-turning gold, and the water murmured its endless, patient sound, and the forest held its breath around us like cupped hands.

But even then, beneath the laughter, beneath the warmth of his skin against mine, beneath the hope that we had left everything behind us—the cathedral, the court, the whispering, the war—I felt it. The shift. The faultline. A wrongness at the edge of things, subtle as a change in air pressure, like the moment before your ears pop. The birds had stopped singing. I hadn't noticed when, but the silence was there now, pressing in from the treeline, heavy and watchful.

Something watching.

When I glanced back at the forest, just for a moment—over Calum's shoulder, past the curtain of falling water—I saw it: a figure between the trees, still and silent, half-swallowed by shadow. It stood where the light didn't reach, its outline wrong somehow, too sharp and too blurred at the same time, like something the eye refused to hold. Waiting. Patient in the way that only predators and the very old can be.

My fingers tightened on Calum's shoulder. The cold crept back in.

And though I could not know it then—though I pressed my face into his neck and breathed him in and told myself it was nothing, a trick of the light, a shadow cast by branches—that was the moment everything began to end.

9

<hr>

The court did not celebrate us. Not truly.

Their faces shifted and flexed into the shape of courtesy the way a mask settles over bone: the smile drawn tight at the corners, the toast raised with fingers that whitened around crystal stems, the words laid out in brittle, practiced arrangements that clinked like glass against glass. They clung to formality as if it might save them, as if the right sequence of bows and murmured pleasantries could stitch the world back into something they recognized. But beneath the surface, something had changed—not broken, not yet, but altered in the way a pane of ice alters when a single fracture threads through it. The shape holds. The light passes through differently. Subtle, but permanent.

I sensed it in the hush that followed us into rooms, the way sound pulled back like a tide when we crossed a threshold. In the way conversation guttered out when Calum turned his head—not sharply, not with threat, just turned it, the way anyone might—and still the nearest cluster of courtiers went quiet mid-syllable, their laughter dying in their throats like snuffed wicks. I sensed it in the way my father's gaze no longer landed on me but passed through, sliding across my face the way light slides across water, touching nothing, as if seeing something behind me that had already been hollowed away.

"They're quieter," I said, voice low, barely louder than the rustle of silk against the marble column I leaned against. The stone was cold through the fabric at my shoulder.

"They're afraid," Calum answered, the same way someone might observe that the wind had shifted, or that the candles were burning low. A fact. Unremarkable.

I looked at him sidelong. The candlelight caught the edge of his jaw, the sharp architecture of his cheekbone. His hands were loose at his sides, utterly still, the way a blade is still before it moves. "Of you?"

A flick of his eyes—dark, quick, a bird changing direction mid-flight. The faintest shadow of a smile pulled at one corner of his mouth, not quite real, not quite reaching anything behind it. "Yes."

Perhaps I should have laughed. The sound should have come easily—dismissive, bright, the kind of laugh that smooths things over. I didn't. My throat stayed closed around it.

We stood at the edge of the great hall, where the vaulted ceiling dissolved into shadow and the last of the firelight couldn't quite reach. The remnants of the feast lay scattered before us across the long tables: goblets of wine half-drunk and left to sour, the dark liquid throwing back a dull, tarnished reflection of the chandeliers above. Fallen petals—white, mostly, though some had been pink before the evening crushed the color from them—lay bruised into the grain of the wood, leaving faint wet stains like old wounds. Candle wax had frozen mid-drip in strange, translucent stalactites along the iron candelabras, each one a record of some hour that had passed without anyone noticing. The air smelled of cold tallow and overripe fruit and something underneath it, something green and sharp, like sap from a branch that had been broken.

It should have felt like the end of something bright. A wedding feast, guttering out. Instead, it was the beginning of something fragile, already splintering, the first hairline crack running through porcelain that everyone would pretend not to see.

"Do you regret it?" he asked, so softly it barely broke the air. The words were almost lost beneath the distant sound of a door closing somewhere deep in the palace, the echo rolling through stone corridors like a held breath finally released.

I turned to him. His face was half in shadow, half in the amber wash of dying firelight, and in that divided light he looked like two people—one I knew, one I was still learning. "No."

His gaze searched mine, moving across my eyes the way a hand moves across a wall in darkness, looking for the crack, the give, the place where the truth might be hiding behind the surface. Sharp as broken glass, that gaze. It could cut if you weren't careful. "Not even a little?"

I took a breath. The air tasted of smoke and cold stone and the fading sweetness of mead. I moved closer, close enough to feel the warmth radiating from his chest through the thin space between us, close enough to see the pulse beating once, twice, in the hollow of his throat. "Not even for a second."

The tension in his shoulders eased—infinitesimal, a fraction of a degree, the kind of shift you'd miss if you weren't watching for it, if you hadn't learned to read the architecture of his body the way a sailor reads the sky. But I saw it. The way the line of his trapezius softened, the way the tendons in his neck released their hold. I saw it.

"Good," he said.

The word hung in the air between us. Not relief. Something heavier, thick as smoke from a fire that had been burning too long in a closed room. It settled on my skin. I could almost taste it—metallic, warm.

"How touching."

The voice was a blade behind us, slid between ribs with surgical precision. I didn't turn. My spine stiffened, each vertebra locking into place, but I didn't turn. I already knew the timbre, the practiced drawl, the way each syllable was shaped to wound while wearing the disguise of wit.

Lord Eryx.

His footsteps were deliberate on the marble, each one placed with the care of a man who wanted you to hear him coming. I caught his scent before I saw him fully—bergamot and something colder underneath, like iron left out in rain.

"I had wondered how long it would take for the Seelie heir to forget her duty," he said. He stood behind us and slightly to the left, close enough that I could feel the displacement of air as he adjusted the fall of his cloak over one shoulder. His voice carried the particular cruelty of someone who has rehearsed their lines.

"I haven't forgotten anything," I replied, steady. My hands were still at my sides. I made sure of it—made sure nothing in me gave him the satisfaction of a flinch.

His gaze slid past me like oil across water, landing on Calum with the weight of something deliberate, something meant to be felt. "No? From here, it looks very much like you've traded your birthright for... *this.*"

The pause before the word was a weapon. The word itself was another. He let it sit there—small, venomous, wrapped in silk.

The silence that followed was ugly, deliberate, swollen with things none of us would say. It pressed against the walls.

Somewhere across the hall, a servant set down a tray too hard, the clatter of silver ringing out and dying instantly, as if the sound itself was afraid to linger.

I stepped forward. My heel struck marble, and the click echoed. "You will choose your next words carefully."

Eryx's smile was thin as a scar, a white line drawn across the lower half of his face that touched nothing above it. His eyes stayed flat, two polished stones. "Or what?"

Calum moved.

Not with speed—with certainty. With inevitability. The way a shadow moves when the sun shifts. One moment at my side, the next, his hand closed around Eryx's throat, fingers settling into place with the ease of something practiced, something that fit. His arm didn't shake. His breathing didn't change.

All sound vanished. Not slowly, not a gradual dimming. At once. As if someone had pressed a hand over the mouth of the entire hall. The remaining courtiers froze mid-gesture—a woman with her goblet halfway to her lips, a man with his hand extended in conversation, fingers still spread, arrested. Even the candle flames seemed to hold, their flicker stilled.

Eryx clawed at Calum's wrist, his manicured nails scraping against skin, leaving thin white lines that didn't bleed. His face darkened, blood pooling beneath the surface, his mouth working around sounds that couldn't find enough air to become words. His boots scraped against the marble, heels searching for purchase. Calum hadn't tightened his grip. Not yet. He held Eryx the way you might hold a door—keeping it exactly where it was, no more, no less.

"Say it again," Calum said. His voice had been stripped down to its components—wire and ice and something beneath both, something that hummed at a frequency I felt in my molars more than heard.

At his feet, the shadows woke.

They didn't creep. They moved the way spilled ink moves across parchment—fluid, hungry, spreading in tendrils across the white marble, darkening the veins in the stone until the floor looked like a living thing, pulsing. The nearest candles guttered, their light shrinking, the warm amber retreating to a tight blue point before steadying, barely holding.

"Calum," I said, but his attention was fixed on Eryx's reddening face, on the pulse hammering visibly beneath his thumb. His jaw was set, the muscles along its edge drawn into sharp relief, and his eyes—his eyes had gone still in a way that was worse than anger. Anger moves. This didn't.

"Say it again."

The darkness grew. It climbed the base of the nearest column, flexing against the carved stone like fingers testing a grip. The temperature dropped—not dramatically, not enough to see breath, but enough that the bare skin of my arms prickled and tightened. The air tasted different. Metallic. Old. Like a door had been opened to a room that had been sealed for centuries.

"Calum."

No answer. The thing inside him was deepening, settling into its own weight like water finding the lowest point. I could see it in the way his pupils had swallowed the color of his irises, in the way the shadows at his feet responded to his breathing—expanding when he inhaled, contracting when he exhaled—as if they were an extension of his lungs.

And that was when I felt it: not fear of him—never that, never once that—but fear of what might happen if I wasn't here to draw him back. Fear of the distance between where he was and where he could go, and the narrowing margin of my voice to close it.

I stepped forward. My hand found his—the one wrapped

around Eryx's throat—and I laid my palm over his knuckles. His skin was cold. Not cool. Cold, the way stone is cold, the way deep water is cold. I pressed my fingers into the spaces between his and held.

"Let him go."

For a heartbeat, nothing changed. The shadows held. Eryx's eyes bulged, capillaries breaking in the whites, tiny red blooms spreading like ink in water. Calum's grip didn't waver. The hall didn't breathe.

Then, slowly—slowly, the way dawn comes, not all at once but in degrees—he turned to look at me. His gaze traveled from Eryx's face to my hand on his, then up my arm, my shoulder, my throat, my mouth, my eyes. The world tilted back into place, degree by degree, like a ship righting itself after a wave.

His fingers loosened. One by one. Eryx dropped to the floor, his knees striking marble with a crack that made someone across the hall flinch. He scrambled away on his hands, coughing, gasping, each breath a torn, ragged thing dragged through a throat that was already swelling. Alive. Barely dignified enough to qualify.

The shadows retreated. They pulled back the way a tide pulls back—reluctantly, leaving the marble wet-looking and dark for a moment before the stone returned to its usual white. The room inhaled. Candle flames straightened. Someone's goblet clinked against a table. No one spoke. No one dared. The silence wasn't the absence of sound—it was the presence of something else, something that had weight and texture, something that pressed against eardrums like deep water.

Because they had seen it. Every courtier in that hall, every servant frozen in the doorway, every member of the council who had been pretending not to watch from the gallery above. They had seen it.

So had I.

Calum straightened. He rolled his shoulders once, a small, precise motion, then dusted his cuffs—left, then right—adjusting the dark fabric where Eryx's clawing had rumpled it. The gesture was so ordinary, so mundane, that it was almost worse than the violence. As if what had just happened required no more recovery than a crease in linen.

"Apologize," he said. Flat. The word had no inflection, no heat. It was an instruction, the way you might tell a dog to sit.

Eryx didn't hesitate. His mouth opened, the bruise already blooming across his throat in shades of violet and black, his voice a ruin of what it had been. "Leave."

And he did. He gathered himself from the floor with hands that shook, turned, and walked—not ran, though every line of his body wanted to—toward the far doors. His dignity trailed behind him like a torn hem, shredded and dragging across the marble, and no one moved to help him. No one even looked.

Calum took my hand. His fingers were warming again, slowly, blood returning to wherever it had gone. "Come."

We walked out. Our footsteps echoed in tandem—mine lighter, quicker, his measured and unhurried—across the hall's expanse. Behind us, the great doors swung shut with a sound like a seal pressing into wax. Final. Airtight.

The corridor beyond was empty. Cold. The stone walls rose on either side, pale and veined with silver, lit by sconces that burned low and blue, casting long shadows that lay flat and still and behaved as shadows should. The hush of aftermath settled on everything—on the flagstones, on the tapestries that hung motionless in air that had forgotten how to move, on the two of us, walking side by side through the silence we had made.

"You didn't lose control," I said. My voice sounded strange in the corridor—too clear, too close, as if the walls were leaning in to listen.

"No."

"You chose to stop."

"Yes."

"Why?"

He didn't even pause. Didn't slow his stride, didn't turn his head. The answer came the way breathing comes—automatic, essential, beneath thought. "Because you asked me to."

Something shifted in me. Not in my chest—deeper. In the place where instinct lives, where the body knows things before the mind names them. A tectonic thing, slow and enormous, grinding plates of certainty against each other until the landscape rearranged.

"And if I hadn't?"

A beat. The space between one footstep and the next, a silence that lasted exactly long enough to be honest.

"I wouldn't have."

The truth lay between us on the cold stone floor, heavy as iron, heavy as a body. Neither of us stepped over it. Neither of us looked away.

"I don't regret it," he said. His thumb moved across my knuckle—once, a small circuit, almost absent.

"I know."

"I only stopped for you."

I believed him. Every syllable, every shade of what it meant. I believed the way you believe gravity—not because someone explained it, but because you've felt it pull. That was the problem. That was exactly the problem.

"You don't have to be afraid of me," he said, and his hand lifted to my cheek. His palm was warm now, fully warm, and his fingers curved along my jaw, his thumb resting just below my eye, where the skin was thinnest, where the pulse of small veins made the flesh tremble. The touch was careful. Deliberate. The touch of someone who knew precisely how much force his hands could apply and was choosing, consciously, to apply almost none.

"I'm not afraid of you." I exhaled, and the breath left me in a thin white cloud that dissolved against his wrist. "I'm afraid of what happens if I'm not here."

His eyes flickered—a contraction of something behind them, a door opening and closing too fast to see what lay beyond—and in that space, the air changed.

It thickened first. Then cooled. Then began to hum, a vibration I felt not in my ears but in my sternum, in the roots of my teeth, in the fine bones of my wrists. Magic gathering—not the bright, warm magic of the Seelie court, not the living magic of root and bloom and sunlit water. This was old. Cold. Absolute. It pressed against the walls of the corridor like a tide against a dam, and the sconces guttered, their blue flames bending sideways as if blown by a wind that wasn't there. The tapestries stirred, their embroidered figures rippling, and somewhere deep in the stone beneath our feet, something groaned.

Calum's grip tightened on my hand. His fingers interlaced with mine and squeezed—not gently, not painfully, but with the urgency of someone anchoring themselves to the only solid thing in a shifting world. His head turned toward the far end of the corridor, where the darkness had begun to move differently—not shadows this time, but light, gathering and building, a cold golden radiance that pulsed like a heartbeat.

"Stay behind me."

But I didn't. I stepped forward, shoulder to shoulder with him, my hand still locked in his. The stone was vibrating beneath my feet now, a fine tremor that traveled up through my ankles, my shins, my spine.

Ahead, the great doors at the corridor's end opened—not swung, not pushed, but parted, as if the stone itself had decided to move. They ground apart with a sound like millstones, and the light poured through, harsh and ancient, carrying with it the smell of crushed metal and something older still, something that smelled the way a lightning-struck oak smells—charred and alive at once.

Oberon entered.

He filled the doorway the way a storm fills a valley—not with size, though he was tall, taller than I remembered, but with presence, with the sheer gravitational weight of power held for centuries. His armor was not armor but light shaped into the suggestion of it, gold and white and burning at the edges, and his face—my father's face—was carved into something I had never seen him wear. Not anger. Something past anger. Something that had burned through anger and come out the other side into a cold, absolute certainty.

The council flanked him. Six of them, robed in silver, their faces arranged in identical expressions of grim purpose. Judgment was written in every line of them—in the set of their mouths, in the rigid angles of their shoulders, in the way their hands were folded precisely at their waists, as if holding something invisible in place.

"This ends now," Oberon said. His voice didn't echo. It pressed. It filled the corridor the way water fills a vessel, finding every corner, every crack, leaving no space untouched.

Calum shifted—just enough to shield, his shoulder moving in front of mine by an inch, maybe two. A geometry of protection so slight it might have been unconscious. Might not have been.

"You don't get to decide that," he said. His voice was quiet against Oberon's, but it held. It held the way a knife holds against a hammer—different force, different kind.

"I already have."

The air was growing dense. Each word landed with physical weight, pressing against my chest, making my lungs work harder. I could feel the magic in the walls now—Seelie magic, the deep magic of the court itself, woven into every stone, every beam, every inch of this place—responding to Oberon's will, tightening like a fist.

"You have brought instability into this realm," Oberon said. His eyes were on Calum, and they burned—not metaphorically, not poetically, but actually burned, a pale fire behind the iris that threw light across his cheekbones. "Violence. Ruin."

Calum's laugh was a hollow thing, scraped from the bottom of something stone and dry. It had no warmth, no humor. It was the sound a tomb might make if it could speak. "You think this is ruin?"

The shadows rose again. They peeled from the floor, from the walls, from the spaces between the sconces, gathering around Calum's feet and climbing his legs like vines. The cold deepened. Frost crept across the nearest wall in delicate, crystalline patterns, each one branching and rebranching in shapes that looked almost like letters in a language I couldn't read.

"This is restraint."

The word landed. I watched it hit the council—watched it move through them like a shudder, each one reacting in sequence: a swallowed breath, a tightened jaw, a hand that moved involuntarily toward a concealed weapon. I saw fear in them. Real fear. The kind that lives in the body, not the mind— the kind that makes the skin go cold and the bowels loosen. It was almost a relief. At least it was honest.

"You see?" Oberon spat. A fleck of light left his lips with the word, dissolving in the air between us.

"I see a king who would cage his own daughter," Calum returned. His voice had dropped, each word weighted and deliberate, placed with the precision of stones in a wall. "She was mine before you defiled her with your name."

The corridor trembled. A crack appeared in the marble to my left, thin as a hair, running from wall to wall.

"I chose him," I said.

The words left me and rang out against the stone, clear and final as a bell struck once. They filled the space Oberon's magic had been pressing into, and for one instant—one breath—everything stopped. The light. The shadows. The trembling stone. All of it, suspended.

"I chose him knowing exactly what he is."

Oberon's jaw worked, the muscles bunching and releasing beneath skin that had gone the color of old parchment. His eyes—my eyes, the same shade, the same shape, the same stubborn fire—were hard as polished agate. "You are not thinking clearly."

"I have never been clearer."

"You have been influenced."

"I have been loved."

The word detonated in the silence. I felt it move through the council, felt it land on each of them differently—a wound, a shock, an accusation. Oberon's nostrils flared. His chest expanded with a breath that seemed to draw all the remaining warmth from the corridor.

He raised his hand.

And the world shattered.

Light ripped across the marble in jagged, blinding lines—not warm light, not the gold of hearth or sun, but the white-hot brilliance of something fundamental being torn apart. The corridor split. Magic tore through the stone the way lightning tears through a tree, and the walls buckled outward, cracks racing through ancient mortar, dust and fragments of crystal raining from the ceiling. The sound was not a sound—it was a pressure, a concussive force that hit my chest and drove the air from my lungs.

Calum moved without thought. His shadows crashed into the golden brilliance with a sound like a thousand panes of glass breaking at once, darkness and light colliding in a roiling, churning wall of force that threw sparks of both into the air. Where they met, the marble beneath them simply ceased—not shattered, not melted, but erased, leaving a void of nothing that the eye refused to process.

"Do not," Calum warned, and his voice was a growl now, something dragged up from a place that had never seen light, vibrating in frequencies that made the remaining intact stone hum in sympathy.

But Oberon pressed forward, relentless, each step sending another pulse of light through the corridor, each pulse brighter than the last. The air tasted of burning—not wood, not flesh, but something elemental, something that had no name. "You will not remain in this realm."

His words were a sentence, already cast—not a threat, not a promise, but a verdict, spoken with the weight of a king who had been making worlds obey for longer than most civilizations had existed. I felt the magic in them. Felt the words sink into the fabric of the corridor, into the stone, into the air, into the Veil itself, reshaping reality with the blunt force of absolute authority.

"What are you doing?" I demanded. My voice cracked against the noise, against the pressure, against the light that was so bright now I could see the bones of my own hand when I raised it to shield my eyes, a red lattice beneath translucent skin.

"Saving you."

"I don't need saving!"

"You do."

Two words. Spoken with the terrible gentleness of a parent who has already decided and is no longer listening.

The Veil split.

I felt it before I saw it—a tearing sensation in the center of my chest, as if something stitched to the fabric of this world was being pulled loose. Then I saw it: a chasm yawning open in the floor between us, not a crack but an absence, a wound in the architecture of reality itself. Cold poured from it—not winter cold, not stone cold, but the cold of void, of between, of the space where no world exists and no light has ever been. It was endless. Looking into it was like looking into the space between stars.

"London," Oberon said.

The word struck heavy, wrong, a stone dropped into water that was too still. It didn't belong here—not in this corridor, not in this realm, not in any sentence spoken by a Fae king in armor made of light. It was a mortal word. A mortal place.

"The mortal realm."

My breath caught, snagged on something sharp in my chest and held there, a fish on a hook.

"You will live there," he said, and each word was a nail driven into the Veil, pinning it open, shaping the wound into a door, "and you will not return."

Inside me, everything stilled. Not calm. Not peace. The stillness of a body in free fall, the moment between the edge and the ground, when gravity has claimed you but the impact hasn't come.

Calum laughed.

The sound did not belong to any mortal throat. It was layered—three voices, five, a dozen, each one at a different pitch, each one carrying a different shade of fury. It filled the corridor and pressed against the walls and made the frost on the stone crack and re-form in new, more violent patterns.

"You think you can exile me?"

The darkness burst outward. Not the controlled, deliberate

shadows of before—this was wild, vicious, a living thing with its own hunger. It tore across the marble in every direction, climbing walls, swallowing sconces, extinguishing light with the indifference of a wave swallowing a shore. Stone shattered where it touched—not cracked, shattered, reduced to powder and fragments that hung suspended in air that had become too thick to let them fall. Someone screamed. One of the council—I couldn't see who—a high, thin sound that cut off abruptly, whether by choice or force I couldn't tell.

"I will tear this realm apart before I let you—"

"Calum."

He didn't hear. The darkness was a roar around him now, a maelstrom of shadow that whipped his hair across his face and pressed his clothes flat against his body. His eyes were open but unseeing—not blind, but looking at something else, something deeper, something behind the surface of the world.

"Calum."

Still nothing. My voice disappeared into the storm of him, swallowed like a match thrown into a furnace.

The rift widened. Reality strained to hold—I could feel it, the way you feel a rope beginning to fray, fiber by fiber, each snap a tiny vibration that adds up to catastrophe. The edges of the chasm were ragged, flickering, and through them I could see glimpses of something grey and wet and impossibly mundane—rain on concrete, the yellow blur of streetlights, the distant wail of a siren in a world that had no idea what was about to fall into it.

I stepped in front of him.

The shadows hit me—cold, so cold, cold enough to burn, pressing against my skin with the weight of deep ocean. I gasped, and the air tasted of ash and iron and old, old dark. But I didn't stop. I seized his face in my hands—his skin was ice, his jaw rigid, the muscles beneath my palms locked and trembling with the force of what was moving through him—and I forced him to look at me.

"Look at me."

His eyes were wrong. Too dark—the irises had been swallowed entirely, and what looked back at me was not empty but full, overfull, a darkness that contained multitudes, that went down and down and down like a well with no bottom. Too distant. He was in there, somewhere, but the distance between us was measured in something other than inches.

"Stay with me."

The shadows faltered. A tremor, nothing more—a hesitation in their relentless expansion, like a heartbeat skipping.

"They're sending us away," I said. My thumbs pressed against his cheekbones. I could feel the cold radiating from his skin, could feel the darkness pushing against my palms like a living thing trying to get between us.

"I don't care."

His voice was still layered, still wrong, but the words were his. Underneath all of it, the words were his.

"I do."

Silence. The shadows held, neither advancing nor retreating, suspended in the space between his fury and my voice.

"If we fight this... you won't stop."

He became still. Utterly still. The kind of stillness that is not the absence of motion but the presence of everything motion could become, held in perfect, terrible balance. The shadows stopped moving. The darkness stopped breathing. Even the rift in the floor seemed to pause, its edges ceasing their ragged flicker.

"And if you don't stop—"

I left the ending unsaid. It hung in the air between us, shapeless and enormous. He understood. I saw it arrive in his eyes—the darkness receding just enough for something else to surface, something raw and human and terrified. Not of Oberon. Not of exile. Of himself.

"I will find you anywhere," he whispered. His voice was his own again—single, stripped bare, shaking at its edges.

"I know."

"I only need you."

"Then choose me."

A breath. A heartbeat. The two sounds so close together they might have been the same.

The shadows trembled—a full-body shudder that passed through every tendril, every thread of darkness—and then, slowly, as if each one required a separate act of will, they drew back. They curled away from the walls, released the shattered stone, retreated from the marble, pulling inward and inward until they were nothing—just the ordinary shadows that belong to a man standing in a corridor, thrown by firelight, behaving as shadows should.

He was himself again. Not safe. Not whole. His skin was still too pale, his breathing still too ragged, and his hands, when they found mine, were shaking with a fine, continuous tremor that he couldn't quite control. But here. Present. The eyes that looked at me were his—dark, yes, always dark, but with the depth of a person behind them, not a void.

His hand closed around mine. His fingers threaded through my fingers and held, and I could feel his pulse in his palm, rapid and hard and alive.

"Together."

"Always."

Oberon wasted no time.

The moment the shadows cleared, his magic surged—a wall of golden light that hit us like a wave, warm and blinding and irresistible. The world tore open. The rift widened beneath our feet, and the cold rushed up, and the grey, rain-soaked glimpse of London expanded into a doorway, into a mouth, into a fall. The light pressed us toward it—not violently, not painfully, but with the absolute certainty of gravity, of tide, of a decision that had already been made by someone who would not unmake it.

I gripped Calum's hand. He gripped mine.

As the light swallowed us—as the marble disappeared beneath our feet and the corridor dissolved and the last thing I saw was my father's face, rigid and burning and utterly convinced of his own righteousness—I knew, too late, the secret the council could not name. The thing they had felt in that hall, in the silence after Calum's hand had closed around Eryx's throat, in the shadows that climbed the walls like living things, in the darkness that answered to his breath.

They hadn't destroyed the threat.

Only sent it somewhere else.

10

I woke cold.

Not the cold of winter air, or water, or wind—a deeper chill, marrow-deep, a weight that pressed into bone and pooled there, refusing to lift. It sat in the joints of my fingers, in the hollows behind my knees, in the shallow dip at the base of my throat where my pulse beat sluggish and thin. For a long moment, I did not move. I did not open my eyes. My body lay heavy against something flat and hard, and even the small effort of breathing felt like dragging air through wet cloth.

The last memory shimmered against the inside of my skull: warmth. Water. The river catching late afternoon light in copper sheets, Calum's hands moving over my skin—his thumb tracing the line of my collarbone, his palm settling warm and sure against the curve of my ribs. His voice threading into my ear, low and unhurried, the way it got when he thought no one else could hear. *We've got time.*

My lips parted. Something fragile, almost a smile, almost surfaced—the muscles around my mouth twitching once before the cold pressed it back down.

And then the stone beneath me, unyielding, pressed sharply against the ridge of my spine. A knot of rock ground into my shoulder blade. The cold was not a sensation but a certainty, a geometry—flat planes and hard angles, the kind of surface that had never been meant for a body to rest against. There was nothing soft about it. Nothing that gave. My eyes snapped open.

Darkness. Not complete; a flicker of light somewhere at the edge of the cell, weak and yellowish, guttering against what might have been a sconce or a crack in the wall—just enough to reveal the wrongness of the space. Low ceiling, close walls, the stone slick with a faint sheen of moisture that caught the dim light and held it in thin, greasy lines. The air was thick, unmoving, old, damp—it sat in my lungs like silt. A taste gathered in the back of my mouth, mineral and sour, faintly metallic, like licking the edge of a copper coin. I could not place it, except that it did not belong. It was not the taste of any place I had ever slept. It was not the taste of anywhere I had chosen to be.

I tried to sit up. Pain shot through both wrists—white, electric, immediate—and I gasped, the sound small and instantly swallowed by the stone, absorbed into the walls as though the room had been built to eat noise. My shoulders wrenched back. Iron circled each wrist, cold and biting, the bands narrow but thick, their edges rough where runes had been etched deep into the metal. The runes burned where they met skin—not fire, exactly, but a focused, insistent heat, the kind that sank through flesh and lodged against the tendons beneath. The chains ran back to the wall behind me, each link no wider than my thumb, their reach precisely calculated: enough to allow me to sit upright, to draw my knees toward my chest, but nothing more. I could not stand. I could not reach the door. I could not bring my hands close enough together to touch my own face.

I stared. The runes shimmered faintly in the dark, their glow a dull, sullen orange, pulsing with the rhythm of something that was not my heartbeat. Their heat was steady, almost thoughtful in its bite—not enough to sear, but enough to ensure I could not forget them. Each breath I took shifted the cuffs a fraction, and each fraction sent a fresh thread of pain lacing up toward my elbows.

For a moment, my mind refused to arrange this into reality. The stone, the chains, the dark, the taste of copper and damp —none of it fit. None of it connected to what came before. Hours ago, I had been in his arms. Hours ago, the river had been warm, and the sky had been wide, and Calum had pressed his forehead to mine and laughed at something I couldn't remember now, the sound vibrating against my lips.

"Calum."

The name left my lips, echoing once, thin and uneven, against the stone. It came back to me warped, the vowels flattened, stripped of everything they were supposed to carry. No answer. The silence that followed was absolute—not empty, but dense, packed tight, the kind of silence that has weight.

Memory surged up, all at once, unbidden and bright: the forest canopy shifting overhead in patterns of green and gold. The water, sun-warmed, sliding between my fingers. Calum's laughter breaking loose from his chest, startled and genuine, the way it only ever was when we were alone. The way he looked at me—his eyes steady, his mouth soft, the hard lines of his face gone slack—as if the rest of the world had fallen away and he could not quite believe what was left.

And then—a break. A clean, surgical gap. The memory simply stopped, its edge sharp as sheared metal. One moment the river, his hands, the light. The next: nothing. A whole moment excised and replaced with blank dark, a void where continuity should have been. I reached for it and found only absence, smooth and featureless, like pressing my hand against a wall where a door had been.

My chest constricted—a physical thing, the muscles between my ribs clenching down hard, my lungs suddenly too small for the air they needed. Panic arrived not as a thought but as a force, a wave of adrenaline that flooded my limbs and made me pull hard against the chains before I could think to stop myself. The runes flared in answer, their glow surging bright enough to throw my shadow against the far wall—a hunched, ragged shape I barely recognized. Heat spiked in the cuffs, sharp and punishing, and the skin beneath them screamed. I hissed through my teeth and recoiled, pressing my back flat against the stone, breath coming sharp and shallow in my lungs. My wrists throbbed. I could feel the weals forming already, the flesh swelling tight against the iron.

"Hello?" My voice was rawer than I meant it to be, scraped thin, the edges of it fraying. "Who's there?"

Silence, dense and attentive. Not the absence of sound— the presence of listening. Silence that pressed against my lips, that leaned in close, as if waiting for me to continue. As if something on the other side of the walls was cataloguing each word I spoke.

I held my breath. Counted the beats of my own pulse. One. Two. Three.

Footsteps. Measured, deliberate, approaching from some-where beyond the door—stone on stone, each step placed with the precision of someone who was in no hurry. The sound grew, unhurried, confident. A shadow shifted in the thin line of light beneath the door.

I went still. My fingers curled into fists, the chains clinking softly with the motion. Every sense sharpened—the cold air on my bare arms, the iron's pulse against my wrists, the faint vibration of those approaching steps traveling through the stone floor and into the base of my spine. My jaw locked. I braced for what would follow.

The door groaned open—a deep, grinding protest of old hinges, the sound reverberating through the cell like a held note. Light sliced in, hard and blinding after the dark, and I flinched before I could stop myself, my eyes narrowing to slits against the sudden glare. The walls leaped into high relief: rough-hewn stone, glistening damp, closer than I had imagined. The cell was barely eight feet across.

Oberon stepped through. Tall. Crowned—the circlet sat against his brow the way it always did, as though it had grown there, the pale metal catching the torchlight from the corridor behind him and scattering it in thin, sharp lines across the ceiling. The lines of his silhouette were so familiar that my chest tightened—the set of those shoulders, the way he held his chin a fraction too high, the precise angle of his stance that I had spent my entire life reading for mood, for intention, for the small permissions that determined what I was allowed to say and when.

He filled the doorway. Behind him, the corridor stretched away in a blur of warm light and distant stone, and for one breath I could smell something other than damp—candle wax, cedar smoke, the clean mineral scent of the upper halls. Home. The scent was gone almost immediately, replaced by the cell's close, wet air.

"Father."

The word came out quieter than I intended, roughened at its edges. My throat worked around it.

He did not move toward me. He did not step forward, did not close the distance between us, did not reach for me. He stood exactly where he was, framed in the doorway's light, and he did not look relieved, or angry, or even surprised. His expression was a mask of decision—something settled and locked into place long before he'd opened this door. I knew that look. I had seen it in council chambers, in throne rooms, in the moment before a sentence was passed. It was the face he wore when the verdict had already been reached and the trial was merely theater.

"What is this?" My voice cracked on the second word, a splintering I could not hide and did not try to. The chains shifted as I straightened, their links scraping against the wall behind me.

He waited before answering. His eyes—pale, steady, the same grey-green I saw in my own reflection—flickered over the damage. My wrists first: the iron cuffs, the reddened skin visible above and below them, the faint shimmer of the runes still pulsing their low heat. Then the chains, their length, their anchor points. Then the marks where the iron had already begun its work—bruises forming in deep, mottled purple along the inside of each wrist, the skin at the edges raw and beginning to blister where the runes bit deepest. His gaze moved across all of it with the careful, cataloguing precision of a man inspecting the condition of a tool. Assessment, not concern. Inventory, not empathy. He noted the damage the way he might note a crack in a foundation—something to be aware of, factored in, managed.

"You're safe now," he said.

The words landed oddly, slightly off-center, as though he meant them—as though he genuinely believed that what he was saying and what I was experiencing occupied the same reality. His voice was the voice I remembered from childhood:

low, authoritative, certain. The voice that had once made me feel that the world was ordered and comprehensible.

"What?"

"You're safe."

Calm, measured, each syllable placed with care, as if he were reporting something simple—the weather, the hour, an unremarkable fact.

A laugh burst out of me before I could stop it, hollow as the cell, the sound bouncing off the close walls and returning to me thin and strange. My ribs ached with it. "Safe? I'm chained in a cell."

His expression did not shift. Not a flicker. Not a twitch at the corner of his mouth, not a narrowing of the eyes. He absorbed the words the way stone absorbs rain.

"You were in far greater danger before."

My gut twisted—a slow, nauseating wrench, as though something inside me had been gripped and turned. "What are you talking about?"

His jaw set. The muscle along the hinge of it flexed once, visibly, the only crack in the composure. "Do not pretend ignorance."

"I'm not pretending anything," I said, and my voice came out sharp enough that the chains rang faintly with the tension in my arms.

He drew closer. The movement was controlled, careful— each step deliberate, his weight settling evenly, the way a man approaches something he considers volatile. Two steps. Three. Close enough now that I could see the details the doorway's light had obscured: the tension in the lines around his mouth, deep grooves that hadn't been there the last time I'd seen him, or maybe I'd never looked closely enough. The certainty in his gaze was absolute, immovable, a wall built so high I couldn't see over it. His hands hung at his sides, loose and still—not clenched, not reaching. Simply present. Simply waiting.

"You are no longer bound to him."

Something inside me locked up. The words hit a place beneath thought, beneath logic, somewhere in the animal core of my chest where instinct lived. My breath stopped. My hands went rigid in the cuffs, fingers splayed, every tendon standing taut beneath the skin.

"No."

"You were compromised."

"No."

"You were being controlled."

"No."

"You were being harmed."

"No."

The word tore out—harsh and immediate, ripped from somewhere deep in my diaphragm, loud enough that it rang against the stone and came back to me doubled. My wrists jerked forward against the chains, and the runes flared, and I didn't care. Heat lanced up my forearms and I held his gaze through it, my teeth bared, my breath ragged.

"He never hurt me."

Oberon's gaze went flinty—the pale grey-green hardening, the pupils contracting to points. A stillness settled over him that was worse than anger, worse than shouting. It was the stillness of a man who has already accounted for every objection and dismissed them all.

"You don't understand what he is."

"I understand exactly what he is."

"A monster."

"My husband."

The word hung between us, dense and immovable, occupying the space like a third body. I could feel it there—the weight of it, the shape of it, the way it changed the air. Oberon's face did not change; if anything, the coldness in him deepened, settling into the bones of his expression the way the cold had settled into mine. His chin lifted a fraction. His shoulders drew back by a degree so small it was almost invisible, but I saw it. I had been reading this man my entire life.

"He has twisted your perception."

"No."

"You are not thinking clearly."

"I have never been clearer."

"You were isolated from your court."

"I chose to leave it."

"He manipulated you."

"I chose him."

Each exchange landed like a struck bell—call and answer, claim and denial, the rhythm of it almost ritualistic, as though we were performing something ancient and inevitable. My voice did not waver. His did not soften. We stared at each other across the narrow cell, and the chains between us—the real ones and the invisible ones—pulled taut.

Silence pooled between us, thick and resistant to any intrusion. It gathered in the corners of the cell, pressed against the walls, filled the space between his body and mine until the air itself felt solid. Oberon exhaled—a slow, deliberate release through his nose, his chest settling, his shoulders lowering by the smallest margin. The sound of it was controlled, measured, the way everything about him was controlled and measured. Even his grief, if that's what this was, arrived on schedule.

"I had hoped," he said, and now his voice was almost gentle—a careful, constructed gentleness, the kind that is chosen rather than felt, laid over the words like a cloth over a blade, "that you would see reason."

"You're wrong," I said.

He did not blink. His eyes held mine with the flat, unwavering certainty of someone who has never in his long life been wrong about anything that mattered. "No. You are."

Something inside my chest cracked—just a line, nothing dramatic, nothing that would show on my face. A hairline fracture running through something that had, until this moment, still been whole. Not because I believed him. Because I understood, with sudden and complete clarity, that he believed himself. That he would not be moved. That this was not a misunderstanding to be corrected but a conviction to be endured.

"Where is he?" I asked. My voice had gone quiet, the rawness smoothed into something flat and deliberate.

No answer. Oberon's mouth pressed into a thin line, the skin around it whitening.

"Where is Calum?"

He hesitated—the first hesitation since he'd entered the cell, a pause so brief it might have been imagined, a fractional delay between my question and the arrangement of his response. Then: "He will not come for you."

I went still. The air left my lungs in a slow, involuntary leak, and for a moment the cell was so quiet I could hear the faint, wet drip of water somewhere behind the walls.

"You are no longer his concern."

"That's a lie."

"It is not."

"He would never—"

"He already has."

The words struck, clean and cold as a blade drawn across skin—the kind of cut so precise you don't feel it at first, only the strange coolness of air against something newly opened. I stared at him. His face gave nothing away. Nothing.

My pulse hammered in my ears—a thick, wet rhythm that

drowned out the dripping water, the faint hum of the runes, the sound of my own breathing. I could feel it in my throat, in my temples, in the bruised hollows of my wrists where the iron sat.

"You're lying."

"I am protecting you."

"You're imprisoning me."

"I am saving you."

"From what?"

Oberon met my gaze, unwavering. The torchlight from the corridor behind him caught the edge of his circlet and threw a thin line of light across his cheek, illuminating the set of his jaw, the deep-carved lines of his face, the absolute and terrible conviction in his eyes.

"From him."

The silence that followed was the longest yet. It stretched between us like a held breath, like the moment before a fall, like the space between a lightning strike and the sound that follows. Neither of us moved. The runes pulsed their low, steady heat against my wrists. The damp air pressed close. Somewhere, water dripped—once, twice, three times—each drop landing with the precision of a metronome counting out the seconds.

Because in that emptiness, I knew—with conviction that lived in the root of bone and marrow, in the place beneath thought where the body keeps its oldest truths—that he was wrong. I knew it the way I knew my own name, the way I knew the feel of Calum's hands, the sound of his breathing in the dark, the exact pitch of his voice when he said my name and meant *I'm here* and *I'm not leaving* and *you are the thing I will not lose.*

Calum would come. He would burn his way through courts and realms if he had to. He would tear through wards and walls and every barrier my father could construct, and he would do it not because he was a monster but because that is what love looks like when it has teeth—when it has been backed into a corner and told to be reasonable.

This cell would not hold me. Not for long.

"You shouldn't have done this," I said, my voice so quiet it barely registered in the air—barely louder than the drip of water, barely more than breath shaped into words. But I held his gaze, and I did not look away, and I did not blink.

Oberon's look did not shift. The mask held. The crown caught the light.

"It was necessary."

"No," I whispered. "It wasn't."

He turned. He walked to the door. He did not look back. The door groaned shut behind him, and the light narrowed to a sliver, then a thread, then nothing. The lock engaged with a sound like a bone breaking clean—a sharp, definitive click that echoed once and was gone.

Darkness closed back in. The runes pulsed. The stone pressed cold and unyielding against my spine.

But beneath the fear, beneath the confusion, beneath the cold iron biting into my wrists and the ache spreading through my shoulders and the lingering ghost of his words—*He already has*—something else was taking hold. It started low, in the pit of my stomach, a heat that had nothing to do with the runes. It climbed through my chest, settled behind my sternum, and burned there with a steady, unflickering flame. Not regret. Not doubt.

Rage.

It sat in me like an ember in a closed fist—quiet, patient, gathering. My fingers curled slowly around the chains, the iron links pressing cold into my palms, and I held them. Held them tight. Let the runes burn. Let the iron bite. Let it all mark me, if it wanted to. Every bruise, every welt, every scar would be evidence.

And when Calum Ravenscroft came for me—and he would come, he would come, the certainty of it was a drumbeat in my blood, steady and relentless and sure—the world would know exactly what kind of mistake my father had made.

11

I knew before the alarm. Before the guards began to shout, before the palace quaked, before the first scream tore the air—I knew. The sense of him was sudden, absolute. Magic surging through the kingdom like a pressure change before a hurricane, the kind you feel in the hollows of your teeth, in the spaces between your ribs. A storm out of place and time: violent, ravenous, so alive it made the marrow in my bones ring with recognition. The torch on the wall outside my cell guttered, the flame bending sideways as if flinching, and the shadows pooled and stretched in directions that had nothing to do with the light.

My breath tangled in my throat. "Calum…" The chains at my wrists rattled as I rose, the manacles biting down, iron teeth grinding against the raw skin beneath—skin already rubbed bloody from days of pulling, testing, hoping. I barely felt it. The dungeon walls trembled. Mortar dust slid from the ceiling in thin, uncertain lines, catching in my hair, settling on my cracked lips. The taste of grit and old stone. And somewhere above—a break. Not a crack. A *break*. The sound of it:

sharp, final, like the spine of the palace snapping clean. Silence held for one impossible breath.

Then the screams came.

Not a handful. Not a few. Hundreds, layered and colliding, echoing down the palace corridors until the sound lost its individual voices and became something monstrous, a single, endless shriek of disbelief and agony and terror. They poured down through the stone like water through fractures, filling every corner of the dungeon with the high, animal wailing of people who had never imagined their own deaths. My stomach twisted, bile rising sharp at the back of my tongue. "No," I whispered. He wouldn't—

But I knew him.

I knew the shape of his rage the way I knew the shape of his hands. I'd felt it sleeping beneath his skin on quiet nights, a banked furnace, patient and immense. I'd traced the scar tissue of old wounds he never spoke about and understood what lived underneath. And I knew—had always known—what would happen if someone cut the last tether holding it in place.

The cell door crashed open, the hinges screaming, one bolt ripping free and skittering across the floor. A guard reeled inside—young, one I'd seen before, the one who'd sometimes left an extra cup of water by the bars when he thought no one was watching. Blood smeared down the front of his armor in a wide, dark swath, and his mouth gasped for air like a landed fish. His pupils were blown wide, the whites showing all around. "He's—" he managed. His hand found the wall, fingers scrabbling for purchase. "He's slaughtering everyone—" The sentence never finished.

Something moved in the threshold. A sound like fabric tearing, wet and thick. The guard's body shuddered—a full-body convulsion, his spine arching, his mouth open in a silent shape that might have been a word or might have been nothing at all—then dropped. He hit the stone floor face-first, and he did not move again.

And Calum Ravenscroft stepped through.

Everything in me went silent. My heartbeat. My breath. The trembling in my hands. All of it, suspended.

He was soaked in blood—not splattered, but *drenched*, as if he'd walked through a river of it. It darkened his shirt to near-black, clinging to his chest, his forearms, the long line of his throat. His hands were slicked red to the wrists, the blood already drying in the creases of his knuckles, collecting under his nails. It was on his face—a streak across his jaw, a smear along one cheekbone, dried flakes in the pale hair at his temple. The smell hit me: copper and salt and something deeper, something organic and wrong, thick enough to coat the back of my throat.

But his eyes—

They were still his. Dark and fierce and desperately, furiously *present*. Not empty. Not lost. Burning with something that looked, from this distance, almost like anguish.

"Ottilie," he said, voice rough, scraped raw as if he'd been screaming or swallowing smoke.

I didn't remember crossing the space. I didn't remember my legs moving, or the chains dragging behind me, or the distance between us closing. Only that suddenly his arms were around me, crushing me against the wet heat of his chest, and the chains at my wrists shrieked—a high metallic whine—and then *snapped*, iron links scattering to the floor like nothing at all, like they were made of dry clay instead of metal meant to hold the fae. The broken manacles clattered against stone and I felt the sudden lightness in my arms, the raw air against the wounds beneath.

He was everywhere: hands on my cheeks, tilting my face

up, thumbs dragging through the grime and the tear tracks I didn't remember leaving. Then my arms—his fingers circling my wrists, feather-light now, turning them over, cataloguing the raw red bands where the iron had sat. Then my shoulders, pressing gently, feeling for damage beneath the skin. Searching. Checking. Making sure.

His jaw worked. A muscle in his cheek twitched, once, twice. His nostrils flared as he took in the sight of me—the filthy dress, the bruises on my arms, the hollow I could feel in my own face from days without proper food.

"Did they hurt you?" The words were tight, sharp, bitten off at the edges. He was strung with tension, every muscle bracing, the cords in his neck standing out like ropes. His fingers trembled where they held my face—a fine, barely visible tremor, the kind that comes not from weakness but from the effort of holding something catastrophic in check.

"No," I said. I caught his wrists, trying to steady him. His pulse hammered against my fingertips, wild and too fast. "Calum. Listen to me."

"They chained you." His gaze dropped to my wrists again. Something in his expression fractured—a hairline crack running through the surface of his control. His thumb brushed the raw, weeping skin where iron had eaten into flesh, and his mouth pressed into a line so tight the color left his lips.

"I'm okay."

"They took you." His voice dropped lower, barely a sound, and his eyes moved over my face with a kind of desperate inventory, as though he were memorizing what they'd done to me, filing each detail away in some dark, meticulous ledger.

"I'm okay," I repeated, urgently. I squeezed his wrists. I pressed my forehead against his chin, feeling the stubble there, the dried blood crackling against my skin.

His grip tightened. His breathing was ragged, uneven—

each exhale shuddering out of him, each inhale catching halfway, like his lungs kept forgetting how to work. The magic rolling off his body was a physical thing: it raised the hair on my arms, hummed in the fillings of my teeth, made the air between us taste of something darker, something burnt.

Something inside him had crossed a line, and I could feel how close it was to breaking everything—feel it in the vibration of his bones against mine, in the way the shadows in the corners of the cell were moving, crawling, reaching toward us like living things.

"Calum," I said again, softer. I lifted my hands to his face and forced his gaze to meet mine. His eyes were wet. Not crying—he wasn't crying—but bright with something held back, something dammed. I held him there. "They think you're hurting me. My father, Nora—they told him you were..." The words stuck, catching on the shame and the fury and the absurdity of it, the monstrous lie that had been used to justify all of this. "Abusing me."

A pause. Silence. The torchlight flickered. A drop of blood fell from his fingertip and hit the stone floor with a sound like a clock ticking.

Then a laugh, cold and bright and *wrong*—a sound I'd never heard from him before, something with teeth in it, something that belonged in a place much darker than this cell. His head tilted slightly, and the smile that followed didn't reach his eyes, didn't soften anything. It just sat there on his blood-streaked face like a wound.

"I will kill them all," he said.

My heart dropped. Not a flutter, not a skip—a plummet, straight down through my chest and into the cold stone beneath my feet.

"No."

"They took you from me." His voice was quiet. Conversational, almost. That was worse.

"I'm here now."

"They locked you in chains." His gaze drifted to the broken manacles on the floor. His expression didn't change, but his hands curled slowly into fists at his sides, the knuckles whitening beneath the blood.

"I'm here."

"They thought I wouldn't come." A breath of something almost like wonder, as though the idea itself was incomprehensible to him—that anyone could be foolish enough, arrogant enough, to believe they could take me and face no reckoning.

"I knew you would."

He drew a breath, the air shivering between us, and I watched his chest expand with it, watched the way his shoulders didn't drop, the way the tension didn't leave. If anything, it gathered. Concentrated. His pupils were blown wide, swallowing the dark of his irises until there was almost no color left.

"I'm not done," Calum said.

The words went through me like a blade—clean and precise and devastating. Not a threat. A statement of fact, delivered with the calm certainty of someone describing the weather.

"Calum, stop."

"I can't." He said it simply. No drama, no posturing. Just the truth, laid bare. His hands opened and closed at his sides, restless, like the magic in him needed somewhere to go and his body couldn't contain it.

"Please."

"They deserve this."

"They don't deserve you like this."

For a moment, something in his eyes shifted. The hard, glittering surface cracked, and I saw *him*—underneath all of it, beneath the blood and the fury and the magic that was eating him alive from the inside out. I saw the man I'd married, the one who'd laughed with me in the water on that last golden afternoon, who'd tipped his head back against the current and let the sun find his face, who'd pulled me under and kissed me with river water in our mouths. I saw him, and he saw me seeing him, and for one breath the world held still.

But it was slipping. I watched it go—watched the softness retreat behind his eyes like a tide pulling back from shore, leaving only the wet, dark rock beneath.

"Stay here," he said.

"No."

"Ottilie—"

"I'm not staying in a cell while you destroy everything."

A flicker of approval crossed his face, quick and sharp—there and gone, a flash of the man who had always loved that I refused to bend. The corner of his mouth twitched. Something passed between us, wordless and old.

"Then stay close," he said.

So I followed him into the ruin.

The palace—

Gods.

The palace was in pieces. The golden halls torn wide open, as though something enormous had clawed its way through from the outside. Walls cracked from floor to ceiling, the fractures spreading in jagged webs through stone that had stood for a thousand years. Columns shattered at their bases, toppled across the corridors in great broken lengths, the carved faces of old kings split and scattered. The crystal chandeliers had fallen—I stepped over shards that crunched under my bare feet, glittering in the dim emergency light of guttering wall sconces. Blood smeared across marble that once caught the light and threw it back in warm, honeyed tones. Now the marble was dark, sticky underfoot, the blood already browning at the edges.

Bodies.

Fae, soldiers, courtiers. A woman in silk with her arm bent the wrong way, her mouth still open, her eyes fixed on the ceiling with an expression of absolute surprise. A guard crumpled at the base of a pillar, his sword still in his hand, his helmet caved in on one side. Two figures near the fountain—which was still running, water burbling peacefully over the carnage—tangled together as if they'd been trying to shield one another. People I'd known since childhood. People who'd served at feasts, who'd danced in the great hall on midsummer nights, who'd bowed when I passed in corridors and called me *my lady* and sometimes, when they thought no one could hear, whispered that I deserved better than the cage my father kept me in. Gone. All of them, gone.

The smell was overwhelming. Blood and bowel and the acrid, electric tang of spent magic, like the air after a lightning strike. It sat heavy in the back of my throat, thick enough to chew.

My breath came too fast, too thin. My vision narrowed at the edges, the corridor telescoping, the bodies blurring into shapes I couldn't let myself look at directly.

"Calum—"

But he was already moving, stepping over the dead with a sureness of foot that made my stomach clench—not hesitating, not stopping, not looking down. His boots left red prints on the marble. The shadows moved with him, sliding along the walls in his wake, reaching ahead like scouts. The closer we drew to the throne room, the quieter the world became—not for lack of destruction, but because there was nothing left to destroy. The silence was worse than the screaming. It was the silence of aftermath, of completed sentences, of full stops.

The great hall doors—twenty feet of ancient oak, carved with the sigils of every fae house, bound in silver that had been blessed by the first Seelie queen—exploded inward. Not opened. Not broken. *Exploded*, the wood splintering into a thousand pieces that hung in the air for one suspended moment before rocketing forward. The blast knocked the air from my lungs and sent me staggering, my hand catching Calum's arm. Heat washed over my face. The concussive force rang in my ears like a bell struck too hard.

And then—

We were inside.

The throne room was vast and ruined. The great stained-glass windows that had lined the eastern wall—each one depicting a scene from the founding, the colors so vivid they'd seemed to breathe in the sunlight—were shattered, nothing left but jagged teeth of colored glass in the frames, the evening sky visible through the gaps, bruised purple and red. The throne itself sat untouched at the far end of the hall, gleaming and obscene amid the devastation, as if the destruction had parted around it deliberately. Tapestries hung in burning ribbons from the walls, the smoke curling upward in lazy spirals. The floor was cracked, great fissures running through the mosaic tiles, and through those cracks came a faint, pulsing glow—something deep and wrong, like the earth itself was wounded and bleeding light.

Oberon stood in the center of it all. My father. He was smaller than I remembered—or maybe the destruction around him made him seem that way, diminished, a figure dwarfed by the scale of what had been done to his kingdom. His robes, once white and gold, were stained with blood—not his own, I could tell by the pattern of it, the way it had been flung across the fabric in arcs that spoke of proximity to violence rather than receipt of it. His crown sat slightly askew on his brow. His magic flickered weakly around him like a candle in a draft, pale blue threads that sputtered and died and reformed, barely holding shape. His hands shook. I could see it from across the hall—the fine tremor in his long fingers, the way he held them slightly away from his body, as though he no longer trusted them.

But his chin was raised. His spine was straight. Even now —even standing in the wreckage of everything he'd built—he held himself like a king.

"You bring ruin upon my kingdom," he said. His voice carried across the hall, amplified by the acoustics of the vaulted ceiling, but I heard the fracture in it. The hairline break beneath the authority.

Calum stepped forward, slow, unhurried. Each footstep deliberate, measured, the sound of his boots on cracked tile echoing in the silence. He didn't rush. He didn't need to. The power rolling off him filled the room like floodwater, pressing against the walls, making the remaining glass in the windows hum and vibrate.

"No," he answered. "You did that."

The air closed in, thick with power. I felt it on my skin— Oberon's magic and Calum's, pressing against each other, the space between them charged and volatile, the way the air feels between two storm fronts about to collide. My ears popped. The taste of copper flooded my mouth.

"You took my daughter," Oberon said. His gaze flicked to me—just for an instant—and I saw something in his face that might have been guilt, or might have been possession, or might have been nothing more than the reflex of a man who had always considered me an extension of himself. "She was never yours to take."

The words cracked through the hall, sharp enough to echo.

Calum didn't flinch. Didn't blink. The blood on his face had dried to a dark mask, and beneath it his expression was terrifyingly still.

"She was mine before you defiled her with your name."

My breath stilled. The words landed in the center of my chest and stayed there, heavy and warm and aching.

"Show her to me," Calum said.

And then I was there. No—I wasn't sure how I'd moved. One moment I was behind Calum, half-hidden in his shadow, and the next the air was being ripped from my lungs as an invisible force seized me around the middle and *yanked*. Oberon had dragged me forward with a flick of his wrist, his magic hooking into the remnants of iron still clinging to my skin, pulling me across the cracked floor and into the open. I stumbled, nearly fell. The chains—the broken chains still dangling from my wrists, the manacles still locked even if the links between them had snapped—caught the light. Blood on my dress, my bare feet cut from the glass in the corridor, my hair hanging lank and unwashed around a face I knew was gaunt and bruised. My body was shaking—not from cold, but from the magic pressing in on all sides, from the adrenaline, from the look on Calum's face when he saw me standing there between them like an offering.

Calum went completely still. Not the stillness of calm. The stillness of something about to detonate—every particle of his being suspended in the instant before catastrophic release. His hands hung at his sides. The shadows at his feet stopped moving. Even the air around him seemed to hold its breath.

"Ottilie," he said, voice breaking. The word cracked down the middle, the two halves falling away from each other, and underneath was something raw and desperate and young— younger than he was, younger than any of this.

"Calum."

"You came."

"I will always come for you."

For a moment, hope flared—sharp and bright enough to cut, bright enough to illuminate the ruined hall in a light that had nothing to do with magic or fire. I saw it in his face: the way his lips parted, the way his brow softened, the way his whole body swayed toward me like a plant toward sun. For one heartbeat, we were just us again. Just two people who had chosen each other against the will of gods and kings and every force that had ever tried to keep us apart.

Then Oberon jerked the chain.

The motion was vicious—a sharp, downward yank that wrenched my arms behind me and buckled my knees. Pain ripped through my joints as I crashed to the marble, my kneecaps striking stone with a crack that I felt in my skull. The impact sang up through my thighbones, my spine, my teeth. A cry tore from my throat before I could stop it.

"No!" Calum snarled—not shouted, *snarled*, the sound ripping from somewhere deep in his chest, barely human. His face contorted. The mask of control shattered completely, and what was underneath was something primordial and terrible, something that had existed long before language or civilization or mercy.

"You see?" Oberon spat. His voice had risen, cracking at its upper register. Sweat gleamed on his brow. His hand was wrapped around the chain, knuckles white, and I could feel his magic trembling through the iron—weak, desperate, a man clutching his last weapon. "This is what your love has brought her."

"Let her go," Calum said, voice gone deadly. Low and flat, stripped of everything—anger, pain, hope. What remained was the pure, distilled promise of annihilation, delivered with the quiet precision of a surgeon naming the incision.

"Or what?"

Calum's smile was like ice. Slow. Deliberate. It spread across his blood-darkened face with a patience that made my skin crawl, because it was the smile of someone who has already won and is simply deciding how much to enjoy what comes next.

"Everything."

Shadows ripped across the floor—fast and coiling, black as pitch, moving with a sentience that made them more creature than absence of light. They wrapped around Oberon's throat like fingers, tightening, lifting him off his feet with a smoothness that was almost gentle. His boots left the ground. His hands flew to his neck, clawing at what couldn't be clawed, nails scraping against darkness that gave way to nothing. The chain fell from his grip, clattering to the floor. His face went red, then purple. His mouth opened and closed, fishlike, soundless.

"Death would be a mercy," Calum snarled. His hand was raised, fingers slightly curled, conducting the shadows with the precision of a maestro. His eyes were fixed on my father's face with an intensity that was almost intimate. "And I am not feeling merciful."

My pulse hammered—in my throat, my temples, the raw wounds at my wrists.

"Calum, stop!"

But he didn't hear me. Or he heard me and it didn't matter. He was already inside Oberon's mind—I could see the moment it happened, the way Oberon's struggling body went rigid, the way his eyes rolled back, the way Calum's own expression shifted into something focused and surgical. He was dismantling something. Taking it apart, piece by piece, with the careful deliberation of someone who wanted every moment to be felt.

My father screamed. Not from pain—or not only from pain. From something deeper, something breaking at the foundation of who he was. It was the sound of a mind being opened and forced to look at itself, every cruelty laid bare, every justification stripped away. The scream went on and on, rising in pitch until it became something thin and glassy and barely human.

"Calum!" I shouted. My voice tore at the edges. I was on my feet, stumbling forward, the broken chains dragging behind me.

The air shattered.

Power slammed into the room—a blow like thunder, like the sky itself had clenched into a fist and struck downward. The floor buckled. The remaining windows blew inward. And everything recoiled—the shadows snapping back, the screaming cutting off, the thick pressure of Calum's magic pushed aside like a curtain by something immeasurably larger. Even Calum staggered, his boots sliding on the cracked tile, his hand dropping to his side. Oberon fell to the ground in a heap, gasping, curling in on himself.

Alistair.

He entered the hall like a verdict. He didn't walk so much as arrive—one moment the doorway was empty, the next he filled it, and the balance of the world shifted on its axis to accommodate him. He was tall, taller than I remembered, and ageless in the way that only the truly ancient are—not young, not old, simply *beyond*. His face was carved and impassive, his silver hair unmoving despite the wind that whipped through the shattered windows. His power didn't announce itself the way Calum's did; it simply *was*, a constant and crushing pressure, like the weight of deep water, like gravity itself had opinions.

The hall fell silent. Even the fires on the tapestries seemed to dim.

"Calum," he said. His voice was quiet, but it filled every corner of the room, every crack in the floor, every hollow in the broken walls. "What have you done?"

"What needed to be done." Calum's chin lifted. His shoulders squared. But I saw the way his left hand trembled at his side—a tremor so slight that only someone who had memorized his body would have noticed.

"Look around you."

"I have."

"Not enough," Calum said. His jaw tightened. His gaze swept the hall—the bodies, the blood, the broken beauty of a place that had stood for millennia—and I watched him take it in without regret, without hesitation, with nothing but the cold certainty of a man who believed the math was simple: they had taken me, and therefore everything they had was forfeit.

The ground trembled. A deep, subsonic vibration that I felt in my bones rather than heard. Reality itself seemed to twist— the edges of the room blurring, the light bending, the air taking on a quality of thinness, as though the fabric of the world was being stretched to its breaking point and the void beneath was beginning to show through.

"The Veil is tearing," Alistair observed. His tone was clinical, detached. He might have been noting a change in the weather. But his eyes—ancient, fathomless, the color of storm clouds over deep ocean—were fixed on Calum with something that might have been sorrow.

"Good." Calum's voice was raw. He meant it. Every syllable.

Fear curled in my gut, cold and serpentine. This wasn't stopping. It was only escalating. The cracks in the floor were widening, and through them I could see *down*—not into earth or foundation, but into darkness, a darkness that moved and breathed and *watched*. The temperature in the room was dropping. My breath misted in front of my face.

"Do it, Alistair."

Nora's voice. Thin, reedy, coming from behind me. I hadn't seen her move—hadn't heard her approach—but suddenly she was there, beside me, close enough that I could smell her perfume beneath the smoke and blood: lily of the valley, sweet and cloying, the scent of every childhood memory I wished I could burn. Her face was pale, her lips pressed thin, her eyes red-rimmed but dry. She looked at me the way she always had —with that particular mixture of pity and conviction, the expression of someone who genuinely believed that hurting you was the same as helping you.

Her hands seized my arms. Her fingers were ice-cold, trembling. Cold iron snapped tight around my wrists—new manacles, prepared, *planned*—and the iron bit into the raw wounds already there. Pain burst, white-hot, blinding. The iron sang against my skin, and I felt my own magic—what little I had, what little had ever been mine—gutter and die like a candle flame pinched between wet fingers.

I screamed. "NO—"

The floor split open. Not cracked—*split*, a rift gaping wide at the center of the hall, the marble peeling back like skin from a wound. And beneath it: darkness. Not shadow, not absence of light, but *the* darkness—endless and ravenous, a hunger given dimension, the Void that existed beneath all things and waited with infinite patience for the world above to fall into it. Cold poured from the opening, a cold that had nothing to do with temperature and everything to do with emptiness—the cold of a place where nothing had ever lived or would ever live, where even memory dissolved.

"Calum!"

I lunged for him. The chains caught, Nora's grip tightened, but I threw my weight forward, my bare feet sliding on blood-slicked marble. He lunged for me—I saw him move, saw his hand reach out, saw his fingers stretch toward mine, the blood on his knuckles catching the dying light. For a heartbeat, our hands nearly met. I felt the heat of his skin across the inches between us. I felt his magic brush mine—one last, desperate flare—warm, familiar, *his*.

"I love you!" I cried. The words came out broken, shattered, not enough—never enough for what they had to carry.

"I will find you," he said. His eyes held mine. In them I saw no doubt. No hesitation. Only the absolute, unshakeable certainty of a man making a vow that he intended to keep across lifetimes, across worlds, across whatever lay on the other side of the abyss opening beneath his feet. "I will always find you."

Then Alistair's power struck him.

It hit like a wave—not fire, not lightning, but something older, something fundamental, the raw force of a will that had shaped continents pressing down on a single point. Calum's body seized. His back arched. His mouth opened in a silent cry, and for one terrible instant I saw him fight it—saw the shadows surge around him, saw his magic flare white-hot and furious, saw every ounce of his strength thrown against the tide.

It wasn't enough.

The world shattered. The sound was beyond sound—a tearing, a rending, the noise a universe makes when something is ripped from its place in the order of things.

Calum fell. His hand—still reaching for mine—was the last thing I saw. His fingers, the blood beneath his nails, the scar across his palm from a promise we'd made to each other in a garden that no longer existed. Then the Void swallowed him. Closed over him like dark water. And he was gone.

The rift sealed. The marble knitted together. The hall went quiet.

And as he vanished, I felt something inside myself tear away—not metaphor, not poetry, but a physical sensation, real as a bone breaking, real as a hand being ripped from a hand. A piece of me, ripped loose at the root, dragged down into the dark with him. The place where it had been was not empty. It was *absence*—a wound in the shape of him, raw and open, that I understood, in the silence that followed, would never heal.

12

When the Void closed, silence poured into its absence, vast and brutal as the storm that had just raged through the courtyard. The sound didn't fade—it severed, as though someone had drawn a blade across the throat of the world. For a moment nothing moved. A pigeon, stunned or broken, lay twitching against the base of a fountain. A banner, half-torn from its pole, swung once and went still. The palace itself seemed to hold, the ancient stones contracting around the emptiness, listening to the echo of what had been lost.

The marble was scored in deep furrows, gouged as if something enormous had dragged claws across the flagstones. Cracks radiated outward from the center of the courtyard in jagged, branching lines, and chunks of pale stone had been torn up and flung against the colonnades. Toppled statues lay in pieces—a hand here, a fractured torso there, a stone face split cleanly down the middle, one half staring up with serene indifference.

Bodies were strewn where the wind had flung them, limbs bent at angles that made my stomach clench, faces turned blindly to the cold sky. One of the palace guards lay draped across the rim of the fountain, his armor blackened, fingers still curled around a sword hilt that had melted and reformed into something unrecognizable. The air smelled of scorched metal, underlaid by something sweeter and more terrible—the iron-salt tang of blood pooling between the cracks.

Above, the clouds had gone. Scoured away, as if the storm had consumed itself in the act of closing. Only a thin winter blue arched overhead, brittle and empty, the kind of sky that looked like it might fracture if you pressed against it.

Calum was gone.

The iron chains still seared my wrists. I stared at them—at the dull grey bands clamped tight against the bones, the skin beneath blistered and weeping where the enchanted metal had burned through the first layers, leaving raw pink tissue that pulsed with my heartbeat. I could feel the heat of them, distantly, the way you feel a fire in another room. There was only the void where he had vanished, the space still humming with the memory of rupture, the air trembling faintly like the surface of water after a stone has been swallowed.

The rift.

I could see nothing but the afterimage of him standing there—the way the light had bent around his shoulders, the way his mouth had opened, not in fear but in something closer to recognition, as though he'd known all along this was how it would end.

"Tilly." The name came from far away, muffled as though underwater. Warped. The syllables stretched and softened, barely reaching me through the ringing that had settled deep in my skull.

Alistair, stepping towards me with careful slowness, picking his way over a shattered column as if navigating a frozen lake. His face was drawn, the skin around his eyes tight and grey, dark circles hollowed beneath them like bruises. His expression was trapped between exhaustion and regret—his brows pulled together, his mouth working around words he hadn't yet chosen. His left hand trembled. He tucked it against his side, but not before I saw it. His movements were awkward, tentative, as if he was uncertain of the ground beneath him, as if the courtyard might split open again and swallow someone else.

My chains snapped open without warning. The mechanism released with a sound like a bone cracking, the iron bands falling away with a sharp metallic clatter that rang across the ruined stones. I flinched at the noise. Nora's hand flicked, almost idly—two fingers, a twist of the wrist, a gesture so small it might have been brushing away an insect—and I was released.

The marks on my skin were red and raw, angry welts where the metal had burned, the edges already darkening to a deep bruised purple. Blisters had risen in a perfect ring around each wrist, tight and shining. But it barely registered. My arms felt weightless, strange, as if they belonged to someone else entirely. I flexed my fingers and felt nothing. I did not look at Alistair. I stepped forward, drawn to the place where Calum had been, my boots grinding against grit and debris. The stones there were still warm—I could feel the heat rising through the soles of my shoes—and the air was tinged with the sharp, acrid aftermath of magic and blood, a scent like burnt copper and crushed herbs, something that clung to the back of my throat and would not dissolve.

I crouched. The warmth radiated up through my knees where they pressed against the marble. A single drop, dark as ink, stained the pale stone.

His blood.

Smaller than a coin, perfectly round, already beginning to

dry at its edges. I hovered my fingers over it, close enough to feel the faint residual heat lifting from it, but I did not touch it. Something twisted in my chest, cold and tight, like a hand closing around my ribs and squeezing. I pressed my palm flat against the stone beside the drop and felt the last traces of warmth bleeding away, second by second, as if the courtyard was forgetting him.

Behind me, Oberon's voice was steady, unyielding, carrying across the wreckage with the practiced authority of a man who had given orders over worse. "He's gone."

The finality of it made the world contract, everything narrowing to a single point—the drop of blood, the cooling stone, and the anger that ignited somewhere behind my sternum, small and white-hot.

"You sent him there," I said. The words were leaden. They dropped from my mouth like stones into still water.

Oberon did not answer at first. I could hear him breathing —measured, controlled, the deliberate rhythm of someone who refused to let his body betray him. When he spoke, each syllable was deliberate, placed with the precision of a mason laying bricks. "He forced our hand. He slaughtered my guards. He came for me. He came to start a war."

I stood, my knees protesting, a sharp ache shooting up through my thighs from crouching on the broken ground. I turned to face him. My father stood at the edge of the courtyard, near the colonnade, framed by two cracked pillars. His robes were torn at the shoulder, a smear of someone else's blood across the embroidered silver at his chest. His crown was absent—lost, I supposed, in the chaos. Without it, he looked older. The lines around his mouth cut deeper, and his silver hair, usually swept back with immaculate discipline, hung loose around his temples, damp with sweat. But his posture was iron. His chin lifted. His hands were clasped behind his back, and I knew without seeing that his fingers were locked together so tightly the knuckles had gone white.

"He came because you locked me in my chambers," I said.

"You were compromised."

"I was meeting someone."

"You were meeting a god capable of destroying this entire court."

"He already had."

I gestured at the courtyard—the rubble, the dead, the fountain now running pink-tinged water through a crack in its basin. A flag bearing our house crest lay crumpled in the dust, one corner soaking in a pool of something dark.

Oberon's eyes hardened, the green of them going flat and opaque, like pond water freezing over. The line of his jaw shifted, muscles bunching beneath the skin, rigid as carved stone. "Yes. And now he never will again."

It was a sentence, a condemnation, and it slashed through me—a clean cut, the kind you don't feel until you see the blood.

"You think the Void will hold him?"

"It has held worse."

"You don't know him."

Oberon's mouth thinned, his lips pressing together until they nearly disappeared. A vein pulsed at his temple, slow and steady. "I know enough."

The courtyard, suddenly, felt smaller, pressed in by the ruin —the dead laid out in their terrible stillness, the shattered stone dusted white as bone, the surviving courtiers clustering at the doors like moths drawn to the safety of the interior, their faces pale and disbelieving in the too-bright light. I could see Lady Maren gripping the doorframe with both hands, her elaborate headdress gone, her hair wild around her face. Beside her, a young page was crying without sound, tears cutting clean tracks through the dust that coated his cheeks. All of this had happened because of me. Because of a single kiss beneath a willow tree, the bark rough against my shoulders, his mouth tasting of rain and something ancient.

"He told me he would come back," I whispered.

My father laughed—softly, the sound barely more than an exhale, as if it pained him, as if the act of laughing cost something he couldn't afford to spend. His shoulders dropped a fraction of an inch, the only concession his body would make to whatever was happening behind his face. "The Void does not release prisoners."

"You're certain?"

"Absolutely."

The sky above was too bright, too empty—scrubbed clean of every cloud, every imperfection, a vast and pitiless blue that offered nothing. No warmth. No shelter. The stillness pressed in, filling my ears with the kind of quiet that hums if you listen long enough, the silence of a world rearranging itself around an absence.

"You're wrong," I said, voice barely audible, the words dissolving almost before they left my lips.

He did not respond. His gaze held mine for another beat, then shifted—up, past me, to the place where the rift had been, as though he could still see it. As though he was making sure.

Alistair's footsteps crunched on broken marble, each step sending small shards skittering across the flagstones with a sound like teeth grinding. He stopped close, an arm's length away, careful, positioning himself the way you might approach a wounded animal—weight on the balls of his feet, hands slightly raised, palms open. Like I might shatter. The resemblance to Calum hit me then, sudden and savage—the same jawline, the same dark brows, the same way his shoulders squared when he was bracing for something. But where Calum's eyes had burned, Alistair's were ash. Spent.

"Ottilie," he said, gentle, the full name instead of the familiar. The name he used when things were serious. His voice was hoarse, scraped raw, and I could see the toll of the magic he'd spent—the slight tremor in his hands, the broken capillaries webbing across the whites of his eyes, the way he kept swallowing as though his mouth had gone dry and would not recover. "This was never supposed to happen."

I turned. "You opened the rift."

"Yes."

"You threw him into it."

"Yes."

"You could have stopped him."

"No."

The certainty made everything tilt, the ground beneath me lurching sideways for a fraction of a second, as if the world was about to slide off its axis. I locked my knees. Swallowed the bile that climbed my throat.

"Why?" My voice was raw, stripped of everything but the question itself.

"Because he had already crossed the line," Alistair said. His gaze dropped to the nearest body—a guard, young, barely older than me, his armor caved in at the chest as though struck by something immense. Alistair's throat worked. He looked away. "He killed hundreds today."

"You trapped him."

"He chose violence."

"You gave him no other option."

A sigh. It emptied Alistair visibly, his chest caving, his shoulders curling inward as though the air leaving his lungs had been the only thing holding him upright. He looked away, toward the broken fountain, where water still burbled through the cracked basin with absurd, cheerful persistence. A muscle in his cheek jumped. "You don't understand what my brother is capable of."

I held his gaze when it returned to mine—held it the way Calum had taught me, steady and unblinking, the way you hold a blade. "Yes," I said. "I do."

He flinched, just slightly—a micro-contraction around the eyes, a pull at the corner of his mouth, as if surprised. Or stung. His lips parted, then closed again. I watched his Adam's apple bob.

"You care about him," he said, quiet. Not a question. A realization settling into place behind his eyes, rearranging everything he thought he knew. The color drained from his face by a shade.

I said nothing. I did not look away. The wind stirred the dust between us, carrying the scent of char and winter.

Behind us, Nora approached, her boots silent on the rubble in a way that defied physics. Her silver hair shifted in the pale wind, catching the light and throwing it back like polished metal. There was not a mark on her—no dust, no blood, not a single tear in the deep grey fabric of her robes. She surveyed the ruins the way a cartographer studies a map: methodically, without sentiment, her pale eyes moving from point to point, cataloguing. Assessing damage.

"This is unfortunate," she said. Her voice carried the same weight as a comment about weather.

My hands clenched, nails biting into the raw skin of my palms, reopening the blisters the chains had left. I felt the sting this time. "You orchestrated this."

Her voice was mild, her eyebrows lifting by a fraction—a performance of surprise so polished it gleamed. "Orchestrated?"

"You warned my father."

"I shared concerns."

"You set a trap."

"I prevented a catastrophe."

Anger burned, bright and thin, a blade heating in a forge. My pulse hammered at the base of my throat. I could feel the flush climbing my neck, the heat spreading across my collarbones. "He came because you pushed him."

Nora's eyes were cool—the color of a lake in deep winter, where the ice goes down so far you can't see the bottom. Not a flicker of guilt. Not a tremor. "Calum requires very little encouragement."

She gestured at the splintered marble with one long-fingered hand, the movement encompassing the bodies, the rubble, the blood-streaked stone. A ring on her index finger caught the light—a thin silver band engraved with symbols I couldn't read. "This outcome was inevitable."

"Inevitable?" The word tasted like ash. It coated my tongue, dry and bitter, and I wanted to spit it out.

"Yes."

Her gaze pinned me, unblinking, with the patient intensity of someone who had watched civilizations rise and collapse and rise again. The wind lifted a strand of silver hair across her face, and she did not move to brush it away. "You were always going to choose him."

Cold certainty ran through me—not hers, but my own, a recognition that dropped through my body like a stone through dark water. My spine straightened. "You don't know me."

"I know patterns."

I swallowed. My throat clicked, dry. "And what pattern do you see?"

Nora's mouth twisted, the corners pulling into something

that might have been a smile if it hadn't carried so much weight —almost kindly, almost pitying, the expression of someone watching a story they've read before reach its inevitable page. "The one where a princess falls in love with a monster."

I stepped toward her. Close enough to see the fine lines at the corners of her eyes, the way her pupils contracted against the light, the small scar beneath her left ear that her hair usually concealed. "And what happens next?"

"History repeats itself," Nora said. Her voice did not waver. "Monsters destroy what they love."

Her eyes flicked to the sky—that vast, empty, terrible blue —and lingered there for a moment, as though she could see through it to whatever lay beyond. "Fortunately, this monster is no longer our problem."

The words hung, dense and heavy, in the aftermath. They settled over the courtyard like another kind of dust. Somewhere behind me, a piece of stone shifted and fell, the sound sharp and small in the silence. A courtier coughed. The fountain burbled on.

For the first time since the rift opened, something colder than grief seeped in—slower, quieter, spreading through my veins like frost crawling across glass. A new resolve, sharper and clearer than pain. It straightened my spine. It steadied my hands. I unclenched my fists and felt the blood from my palms run warm between my fingers.

They were wrong. All of them. My father with his certainty, Alistair with his regret, Nora with her patterns and her history. The Void might have swallowed Calum, and the court could believe he was lost—could sweep the rubble and mourn the dead and seal the cracks in the marble and pretend that the world had been set right. But the memory of his promise rang through me, unbroken and fierce, lodged somewhere beneath my ribs where no magic could reach it, where no Void could swallow it away.

I'll come back.

The drop of blood on the marble was drying. Soon it would be nothing—a dark stain, then a shadow, then gone. But I had seen it. I had felt the warmth still rising from the stone.

If the Void would not release him, then I would find a way to break it.

I turned my back on the courtyard and walked toward the doors, my boots crunching over the ruin, the cold wind pressing against my face. No one called after me. No one tried to stop me.

The silence followed, but it no longer felt empty.

It felt like a beginning.

13

The court had learned the trick of pretending. Pretending that nothing had changed at all. That was the first thing I noticed—the careful, almost deliberate way the palace resumed its routines. Three days after the massacre, the fountains in the courtyard ran clear and cold as if nothing had stained the marble beneath them. I stood at my window that first morning and watched two servants on their knees with horsehair brushes, scrubbing at something dark between the flagstones. By noon the stone was white again. The jagged teeth of ruined statues—a satyr missing its jaw, a nymph split clean down the torso—were carted away on cloth-draped litters and replaced with perfect facsimiles, their surfaces still smelling faintly of fresh-cut alabaster. Music filled the great hall that evening, bright and precise as always, a string quartet positioned in the same alcove they had occupied the night everything happened. The cellist's hands shook on her bow. No one mentioned it.

But the silence pressed in on me, heavier than before. Not the absence of sound—there was plenty of sound, the clink of goblets and the rustle of silk and the mechanical pleasantries traded across dinner tables. It was a different silence, the kind that lived underneath conversation, thick as silt at the bottom of a river. No one spoke unless necessity demanded it. The courtiers bowed when I entered a room, their spines folding at precisely the correct angle, but their eyes moved over me with something new. A flinch at the corners. A tightening around the mouth. Not quite hatred. Not just suspicion. I saw it in the way Lady Ashworth's fingers whitened around her wine glass when I passed her chair, in the way Lord Maren's gaze darted to the nearest exit before settling back on my face with a smile that never reached his temples. Fear. I had become a living reminder of what had happened—the god who had torn through the palace like a blade through wet paper, the hundreds dead and the walls still groaning where the stone had cracked, the man my father had thrown into the Void while the chandeliers swung and the court screamed.

My father never spoke of it. Not once. He addressed me during council meetings in the same measured tone, his quill scratching steadily across parchment, discussing alliances and magical trade routes as if the destruction of the Seelie court had been no more than a diplomatic inconvenience. His jaw stayed set. His eyes stayed flat. When I entered the council chamber each morning, he would glance up the way one glances at a clock—noting my presence, registering the time, moving on. But I was no longer permitted to wander the gardens. The paths where Calum and I had walked were roped off, officially for restoration, though I could see from my window that no workers came or went. Guards followed me everywhere: two posted outside my door through the night, their armor creaking softly when they shifted weight from boot to boot, and two more shadowing the council hall, positioned at the far wall where they could watch without appearing to watch. I had been caged, but with courtesy for bars and ceremony as locks. The gilding didn't change the shape of the thing.

It did not change what I needed to do.

The library slept in the western wing, sunk deep into the palace's stone heart, accessible only through a narrow corridor that spiraled downward like the interior of a shell. The steps were worn smooth in their centers from centuries of descending feet, and the walls wept moisture where the rock met the earth. Above, lanterns burned and music drifted and courtiers performed their careful pantomime of normalcy, but here the air was heavy with dust and the sweet-rot smell of aging vellum and the pulse of old magic—a low hum I felt more than heard, like pressing my palm flat against a beehive. The ceiling arched high overhead, lost in shadow. Shelves climbed the walls to vanishing points, their wood dark and warped with age, and the books packed into them were dense as bricks, their spines cracked and faded to the color of old bruises. Guards rarely followed me into the stacks. I'd learned this over the past three days, testing the boundary like pressing a thumb against a bruise—walking slower, lingering longer, noting when the armored footsteps behind me faltered and stopped. Books bored them. The dim light and the close air and the endless, whispering quiet made them restless. They posted themselves at the top of the spiral stairs and let me descend alone. The stacks were the only hiding places I trusted.

I slipped between the shelves with a lantern in my hand, its flame turned low, its light stifled further inside the fold of my cloak so that only a thin amber line leaked out along the floor. My slippers made no sound on the flagstones. The shelves narrowed as I moved deeper, pressing closer together until I had to turn sideways to pass between them, the books' spines brushing my shoulders like dry fingers. The deepest reaches of the library held ancient fae histories bound in leather that had gone soft as skin, the chronicles of empires ground to dust— the Autumn Accord, the Fall of the Thornwall Dynasty, the Silent War that had eaten an entire court and left nothing but a name. And buried beneath those, in a low-ceilinged alcove where the stone floor gave way to packed earth and the air tasted of copper and chalk—the forbidden shelves. The books my tutors had warned me about with tight mouths and care-ful, sideways phrasing. Magics that shouldn't be touched. Rituals that cost too much. Knowledge kings preferred to bury and forget, shoved down here where the damp could do its slow work of erasure. Which meant it was exactly what I needed.

I set the lantern on a stone table scored with old knife marks and ring-stains from a hundred previous lanterns. The flame guttered, then steadied, throwing a circle of warm light that barely reached the nearest shelf. I cracked open the first book. The pages rasped against my fingers, dry and brittle as dead leaves, the ink faded to a rusty brown that could have been old blood. The text was written in High Fae script, the letters sharp and angular, and I had to squint to parse them, mouthing the words silently. My eyes moved quickly.

Void. Prison magic. Divine binding. I turned page after page, the paper whispering beneath my fingertips, each chapter more clinical than the last. Diagrams of geometries that hurt to look at—concentric circles collapsing inward, dimensions folded over themselves like origami made of space. Accounts of those who had attempted retrieval: a queen who had poured her entire court's magic into a summoning circle and succeeded only in pulling back a handful of ash. A god-smith who had forged a key from his own bones and found that the lock had no door. Every passage bled into the next, and all their endings were the same: *Irreversible. Permanent.*

Beyond mortal interference. The words repeated across texts separated by centuries, by authors who had never known each other, arriving independently at the same blunt conclusion like travelers converging on a wall.

I snapped the book shut. The sound shuddered through the quiet, a flat crack that bounced off stone and came back to me altered, thinner.

"He told you he would come back."

The words cut from the darkness behind me. I spun around, my hand catching the edge of the table, the lantern rocking on its base and sending shadows lurching up the walls.

Nora stepped into the lantern's glow. She materialized at the boundary of the light the way a shape resolves from fog— first the pale line of her jaw, then the sharp architecture of her cheekbones, then her eyes, dark and steady and watching me with an expression I couldn't immediately name. She wore no court finery tonight. A simple dark dress, her hair pulled back tight from her face, her feet in soft-soled shoes that explained why I hadn't heard her approach. My pulse jerked, sharp and immediate, a physical thing hammering at the base of my throat.

"What are you doing here?"

She just shrugged, one shoulder lifting and dropping with a casualness that felt rehearsed. "I might ask you the same." Her gaze flicked to the circle of books spread on the table—the open spines, the dog-eared pages, the notes I'd scratched on a scrap of parchment in my own clumsy shorthand. I watched her eyes track across the titles and saw the moment she understood. Something shifted in her face, a softening so brief I might have imagined it. "Researching the Void?" Her voice was almost gentle, the way one speaks to someone standing on a ledge. "That's... ambitious."

"You're spying on me."

"I'm observing you."

"You followed me."

"I suspected you would come here." Her mouth curled, not quite a smile—the corners lifting without any warmth reaching the rest of her face. "Grief makes people curious."

A flare of anger, hot and sudden, climbing my sternum like a flame up a wick. I bared my teeth, felt the muscles in my jaw go tight. "You already know what I'm looking for."

"Yes."

"And?"

"I admire the determination." She stepped closer, and I caught her scent—something herbal and astringent, like crushed sage, underlaid with the faintest trace of smoke. Her fingers brushed the edge of the closest book, tracing the cracked leather of its cover the way one might stroke the spine of a sleeping animal. "Unfortunately, you're wasting your time."

"You don't know that."

"Oh, I do." She tapped the ancient cover, a dry click of nail against hide. "The Void is not a prison one escapes."

"Then why are you here?"

She lifted her eyes to mine. The lantern flame caught in them, twin points of amber in the dark. "Because I want to see how far you'll go before you realize that."

I clenched my fists. My nails bit into my palms, four small crescents of pain on each hand.

"He's not dead."

"No."

"So he can still return."

"That means he is trapped in a place designed to hold gods." The certainty in her voice rang like iron struck against iron, clear and absolute and carrying no room for doubt.

"You don't know everything."

"No," Nora said. "But I know enough." She circled the table slowly, trailing her fingertips along its edge, lantern light flickering across her face and throwing the hollows of her cheeks into sharp relief. She looked thinner than I remembered. Or maybe it was the light. "Do you know what the Void does to those inside it?"

I didn't answer. My tongue pressed against the roof of my mouth, dry and thick.

"It strips them down. Magic. Memory. Identity." She ticked each word off like items on a list, her voice flat and clinical, but her eyes glinted with something that looked almost like pity. "By the time it releases them... if it ever does... they're rarely the same creature that entered."

The words hooked cold through my spine, a physical chill that started at the base of my skull and traveled downward, vertebra by vertebra, until my shoulders drew tight and my stomach clenched around nothing.

"You're lying."

"Am I?"

"You hate him."

"That's not entirely true." She tilted her head, a slow, birdlike motion that exposed the long line of her throat. "I simply understand him."

"And I don't?"

"You understand the man you met in the gardens." She bared her teeth—a real smile, this time, wide enough to show the sharp points of her canines, and for a moment she looked less like a courtier and more like something feral wearing courtier's clothes. "I understand the monster beneath him."

I took a step closer. The space between us shrank to the width of an arm's length. I could see the fine lines at the corners of her eyes, the slight unevenness of her breathing. "You wanted this to happen."

"Wanted?"

"You pushed my father."

"I warned him."

"You provoked Calum."

"That was remarkably easy."

My breath shivered out through my teeth, thin and unsteady. "You manipulated everything."

"Perhaps."

"And why?"

Nora considered. Her gaze drifted away from me for the first time, settling somewhere in the middle distance, and for a moment her face went very still—not composed, but blank, the way a lake goes flat before a storm. "Because Calum Raven-scroft has always been a storm waiting to break."

"And you decided to break him."

"Someone had to."

The words settled, heavy as stone dropped into deep water, the ripples spreading outward through the silence.

I stared at her. Studied the set of her mouth, the tension in the tendons of her neck, the way her hands—which had been so steady a moment ago—now pressed flat against her thighs as if to keep them from trembling. "You're afraid of him."

A soft laugh, barely more than an exhale. "No. I'm afraid of what happens when no one stops him." Her gaze flicked over the books again, cataloguing them with quick, precise move-ments of her eyes. "You're searching for a way to free him."

"Yes."

"You won't find one here."

"Then where?"

She hesitated. The pause lasted only a second, but I watched it move through her body—a stiffening of the shoulders, a tightening around the eyes, a brief pressing-together of the lips as if holding back something she wasn't certain she should release. Then: "If such a method existed…" Her eyes flickered, unreadable, the lantern light sliding across them like oil across water. "…it wouldn't be written in books."

"Where would it be?"

"In bargains." The word hung between us, dense with implication, and the air in the alcove seemed to thicken around it. The lantern flame dipped as if something had drawn a breath.

"What kind of bargains?"

"The kind made in very dark places." She turned toward the stairs, her movement fluid and unhurried, but I caught the way her hand found the wall and pressed against it—steadying herself, or drawing comfort from the solidity of the stone. "There are creatures older than the courts. Older than treaties. Older even than gods."

My heart hammered faster, the blood loud in my ears. "You know who I mean."

Everyone did. The stories were packed in silence and warnings, whispered between children under bedcovers and then never repeated in daylight—a name never spoken outright, as if the syllables themselves might carry weight, might travel, might arrive at ears that were always listening. A being who lived outside the realms, in the spaces between maps, in the margins where the ink ran out. A collector of impossible deals, trading power for impossible prices. I had heard the stories since I was small enough to sit on my nurse's knee, and even then they had the quality of something true—not legend, not myth, but testimony.

"The Witch," I said.

The word dropped into the silence like a coal into snow. Something in the air shifted—or maybe I imagined it. Maybe it was just the way Nora's spine straightened, a minute adjustment, as if a thread attached to the crown of her head had been pulled taut.

Nora's smile sharpened, the edges of it going thin and precise as a blade. "Some call her that."

"And you're telling me to find her."

"No." Nora paused at the top of the stairs, her face half-shadowed where the lantern's reach failed, one eye bright and the other lost in darkness. The damp stone glistened behind her like something alive. "I'm telling you what desperation leads people to."

The stone walls rippled with lanternlight, the shadows bending and stretching as the flame guttered in some imperceptible draft. Nora stood there for a moment longer, poised on the threshold between the library's depths and the world above, and when she spoke again her voice had dropped—soft, almost kind, stripped of its usual sharpness in a way that frightened me more than anything else she'd said.

"Be careful, Princess." A pause, the silence filling with the distant drip of water somewhere deep in the walls. "Because if you go looking for her..." Her eyes pinned mine, dark and steady and utterly, terribly serious. "You might actually find her."

Then she turned and climbed the stairs, her soft-soled shoes making no sound on the worn stone, and within moments the darkness swallowed her as completely as if she had never been there at all. I stood alone in the lantern's shrinking circle of light, the forbidden books spread before me like an accusation, the word *bargain* still ringing in the silence between my ribs.

There were no maps that charted the road to Kakia. That was the first thing I understood.

In the palace library, hundreds of books lined the walls in rows that stretched from the marble floor to the vaulted ceiling, their spines cracked and faded, heavy with the dust of centuries. I pulled them down one by one, my fingers coming away gray and gritty. Tomes on vanished gods whose names tasted like ash when spoken aloud.

Theorems of old magic scrawled in ink that still shimmered faintly, as though the words themselves refused to die. Careful records of war and betrayal, their pages brittle and yellowed, stiff enough to cut skin. I read until my eyes burned and the candles guttered down to stubs of pooling wax.

But not one of them offered a clear path to the being Nora had mentioned with such ease.

The Witch.

The Bargain-Maker.

The Devourer of Oaths.

Every text named her differently. Some referenced her only

in the margins, in handwriting so small I had to press my face close enough to smell the mildew blooming in the binding. Others devoted entire chapters to warnings, the script growing more erratic toward the end, as if the author's hand had begun to shake. Every text concluded the same way:

Do not seek her.

That was enough. If something must not be sought, it exists. And if she existed—

She was the last card left to play.

Three nights after Nora cornered me in the library, I left the palace.

I dressed in the dark, pulling on the heaviest cloak I owned —wool lined with fox fur, the kind meant for riding, not fleeing. My fingers fumbled with the clasp at my throat. I left behind the rings, the circlet, the thin gold chain my mother had given me before she died. Anything that caught light. Anything that marked me as what I was.

Leaving the Seelie court behind was easier than it ought to have been. The guards stationed outside my chambers had grown lax, their postures loose, their heads dipping toward their chests in the slow rhythms of men fighting sleep. They were convinced that grief had hollowed out whatever stubbornness had led me into the gardens before. That the massacre had made me docile, obedient. I'd given them every reason to believe it—eating when told, sleeping when told, sitting at my father's table with my hands folded and my mouth shut.

They were fools.

I slipped past them through the servants' corridor, the one that smelled of lye soap and cold stone, where the walls sweated with condensation and the floor was worn smooth by a century of quiet feet. The palace kitchen was empty at this hour, the great hearth banked to embers that pulsed a dull, sleepy orange. I eased the side door open. The hinges groaned —a low, metallic sound that made my teeth clench—and I held still, counting my heartbeats until the silence settled again.

Beyond the palace walls, the forest greeted me with silence.

Not the comfortable silence of a sleeping house. This was the silence of something vast and watchful, the kind that presses against your eardrums until you hear your own blood moving. Winter had begun to spill across the Seelie lands, coating the gnarled branches with a dusting of silver frost that glittered where the light caught it. The ground beneath my boots was hard, the earth frozen into rigid furrows that crunched with each step. The moon was a low, pale coin behind the trees, its light thin and watery, illuminating the narrow path in patches before it vanished quickly into the darkness ahead.

My breath came out in small white clouds that dissolved against the cold.

I walked alone, and for the first time since Calum fell into the Void, the court was a distant memory. No guards shifting their weight behind me. No gossip hissing through silk-curtained alcoves. No father measuring my worth with every breath, his gaze landing on me like something weighed and found wanting.

Just the quiet woods. The creak of frozen branches over-head. The occasional soft thud of snow sliding from a bough and landing in the undergrowth. And the certainty, settling into my bones like the cold itself, that this was more dangerous than any court intrigue.

The farther I walked, the stranger the forest became.

It happened gradually at first—a wrongness I felt before I could name. The oaks, which had been tall and orderly near the palace grounds, began to twist. Their trunks corkscrewed into impossible shapes, bark splitting into patterns that looked almost like faces if I stared too long. Roots humped up from the frozen ground at strange angles, pale and knotted, grasping at nothing. The branches above wove together so tightly that the moonlight dimmed to a faint, sickly glow, and then to almost nothing at all.

The air thickened. It tasted different here—metallic, faintly sweet, like the residue left after a lightning strike. Magic pressed in from all sides, cold and coiling, sliding against my skin like something alive. The hair on my arms rose. My teeth ached. At some point, the path simply dissolved beneath me— one moment packed earth, the next a tangle of roots and dead leaves and moss so dark it looked black.

I stopped and looked behind me. The way I'd come was gone, swallowed by the same twisted forest that surrounded me on every side.

Still, I kept moving.

Because something ahead was waiting.

I felt it—a prickling along my scalp, a pressure building behind my sternum, a presence like a whisper on the back of my neck. The kind of awareness that makes the body go rigid before the mind catches up. The forest had started to watch. I could feel it in the way the silence changed, deepening into something attentive, something that held its breath. Branches creaked without wind. Frost patterns on the bark shifted when I turned my head, rearranging themselves into shapes I couldn't quite read.

My hand found the knife at my belt. My palm was slick against the leather grip.

"You've come a long way to die, little fae."

The voice smoked through the dark—low, unhurried, curling through the frozen air like something with weight and texture. It seemed to come from everywhere at once: from the branches above, from the earth below, from the space just behind my left ear.

I stopped. My boots ground into the frost. Turned.

Nothing behind me but frost, silence, tangled branches. The trees stood like sentinels, their twisted forms casting shadows that pooled and overlapped until the darkness between them was absolute.

"Turn around," the voice said.

I did.

And there she was.

She sat on a fallen tree in the clearing's center, one leg crossed over the other, her posture easy and deliberate, like a queen holding court in a throne room only she could see. I would have sworn the clearing hadn't been there a heartbeat before—I had been staring into a wall of knotted trunks, and now there was this: an open circle of ground, the frost here thinner, the moonlight somehow brighter, as though the canopy had peeled back to let it through.

She looked young. Younger than I'd imagined. Her face was smooth, angular, with cheekbones sharp enough to cast their own shadows. Black hair spilled over one shoulder in a heavy curtain, so dark it seemed to absorb the light around it. Her dress shimmered with black and silver, like shadows stitched with threads of moonlight—the fabric moved even though there was no wind, rippling faintly, as though something breathed beneath it.

But her eyes were wrong.

They were the color of raw amber, bright and liquid, and they held a depth that didn't belong in a face that young. Too bright, too old. Looking into them was like staring down a well and seeing no bottom—just the distant, cold glimmer of something ancient looking back up.

Power hung around her like a storm. Not the controlled, elegant magic of the Seelie court, all golden light and careful intention. This was wild. I could feel it vibrating in the air between us, pressing against my skin, making the fine hairs on my arms stand rigid. The trees at the clearing's edge leaned slightly away from her, their branches angled back, as if even the forest kept its distance.

"Kakia," I said.

My voice came out steadier than I felt. My hands were shaking. I pressed them flat against my thighs.

She smiled. It was a slow thing, spreading across her face like a crack through ice.

"Princess Ottilie of the Seelie court."

My chest clenched. The muscles along my ribs tightened so suddenly it felt like a fist closing around my lungs.

"You know me."

A soft sigh. Her breath didn't mist in the cold air the way mine did. "Of course I do. I knew you were coming before you ever left your palace."

The space seemed to shrink; the trees leaned closer, their branches dipping inward as though drawn by invisible thread. The clearing, which had felt open a moment before, now pressed tight around us. I became aware of how small I was in this place. How far from anything I knew.

"How?"

"Desperation," she said, "has a very particular scent."

She considered me, head tilted to one side like a bird studying something pinned beneath its talon. Her amber eyes moved across my face, down to my clenched hands, back up. Reading me.

"And you reek of it."

The words landed like a slap, but I didn't flinch. I'd had years of practice at not flinching.

I moved forward, careful. Each step deliberate, weight balanced, the way you approach a predator you cannot outrun. The frost crunched softly under my boots. I kept my hands visible, my spine straight, my chin level.

"I came to make a bargain."

Laughter. The sound ricocheted among the trees, bouncing off trunks and branches until it surrounded me, layered and dissonant, as though a dozen versions of her were laughing at once. A crow—or something shaped like a crow—burst from a branch overhead and vanished into the dark.

"They always do."

"I'm serious."

"So am I."

The laughter died as quickly as it had come. Her face was still, her mouth a flat, considering line.

She gestured for me to come closer. A flick of her fingers, casual, the way you'd beckon a servant. The motion trailed a faint luminescence in the air, a pale afterimage that lingered and then dissolved.

I did.

The ground was strangely warm beneath my boots, even though winter gripped the forest all around. Heat radiated up through the soles of my feet, subtle but unmistakable, as if something smoldered far beneath the earth. The frost at the clearing's center had melted entirely, leaving the soil dark and damp, and I caught the faint mineral smell of wet stone.

"You want something impossible," Kakia said. Her voice was quieter now, stripped of performance. Almost conversational.

"Yes."

"You want someone back."

My throat tightened. The muscles in my jaw clenched hard

enough that I felt the ache radiate up toward my temples. I swallowed against it.

"Yes."

Her smile sharpened. The softness vanished from her face, replaced by something keen and predatory, the way a blade looks when it catches the light at the right angle.

"The god your father threw into the Void."

My hands curled into fists. My nails bit into my palms—four small crescents of pain on each hand, grounding me.

"Yes."

She leaned forward, and the shadows leaned with her, bending toward me as though they were extensions of her body. Her eyes were hungry. Not with appetite—with interest. The kind of focused, burning attention a scholar gives a rare text, or a predator gives prey it hasn't seen before.

"You understand what the Void is?"

"A prison."

"A grave," she said. The word landed heavy in the air between us. "Most who enter never return."

"Calum will."

"Because you want him to?"

"Because I'll find a way."

Her laughter was sharp this time, a single bright crack of sound, like a branch snapping in the cold. She pressed a hand to her collarbone, fingers splayed, and looked at me with something that might have been delight.

"Oh, I like you."

"Good."

She leaned closer. The smell of smoke intensified—woodsmoke, old and deep, layered beneath something sweeter and stranger that I couldn't name. The shadows around her shoulders bent with her, trailing behind like a cloak made of dark water.

"But you misunderstand something."

"What?"

"You can't break the Void."

The words hit the center of my chest. I kept my face still. Kept breathing.

"Then how do I open it?"

"You don't."

She stopped just out of reach. Close enough that I could see the faint, unnatural shimmer beneath her skin, a luminescence that pulsed faintly at her temples and along the line of her jaw, as if light moved through her veins instead of blood.

"You trade for it."

My heart hammered. I felt it in my throat, in my wrists, in the soft hollow behind my ears. The rhythm was too fast, too loud. She could hear it—I was certain she could hear it.

"That's why you're here," she said. Her voice was almost gentle. "You already know the truth."

"What truth?"

"That magic like this always has a price."

"I'm willing to pay it."

Kakia's smile was slow, considering. It spread across her face the way dawn moves across water—gradual, inevitable, transforming everything it touched.

"I know."

She studied my face as if reading it like a map. Her gaze traced my forehead, my cheekbones, the set of my mouth, the tension in the muscles around my eyes. I had the unsettling sense that she was seeing not just my face but everything behind it—every sleepless night, every argument swallowed, every moment I'd stood at the edge of the Void's seal and pressed my palms against the cold stone until my fingers went numb.

"But the question is not whether you'll pay," she said. "It's whether you understand what I'm asking."

I met her gaze, steady. Held it. Let her see whatever she was looking for.

"Tell me."

She moved closer. The air around her smelled of smoke and winter roses—the deep, bruised sweetness of petals frozen on the stem, preserved and decaying at the same time. The warmth rising from the ground intensified, and I felt sweat prick along my hairline even as my breath still misted white.

"You want Calum Ravenscroft freed from the Void," she said.

"Yes."

"I can do that."

Hope burned up in me, bright and desperate—a flare behind my ribs that made my vision blur for half a second. I blinked hard. My fingers trembled at my sides. I pressed them against my thighs to still them.

"But nothing that powerful comes without a cost."

"I understand that."

She shook her head, almost tender. The gesture was small, a bare movement, and something in her expression shifted—a flicker of what might have been pity, or recognition, or both. "No, you don't."

Her fingers twitched at her side—a subtle, involuntary motion, like a pianist's hand remembering a chord. A ripple of magic ran through the clearing. I felt it pass through me: a wave of pressure that started in my chest and radiated outward, making my bones hum. The frost at the clearing's edge crackled and reformed into new patterns. The branches overhead groaned and shifted.

"You love him."

Not a question. A statement, flat and absolute, the way you'd state the color of the sky.

"Yes."

The word came out rough. I didn't try to smooth it.

"And he loves you."

The truth hit harder than I'd expected. Not because it was new—I'd known it, carried it, turned it over in my hands during every dark and sleepless hour since he'd fallen. But hearing it spoken aloud, here, in this clearing that shouldn't exist, by this creature who shouldn't be real—it made the knowing sharper. It pressed against something bruised and raw inside my chest, and for one terrible moment my eyes burned.

I didn't blink. I didn't look away.

"Yes."

Kakia's smile was all teeth. White and even and faintly luminous, too many of them somehow, though when I looked again the count seemed normal. The smile didn't reach her eyes. Her eyes had gone very still, very focused, the way a flame goes still in the instant before it catches.

"Good."

"Why?"

"Because love makes people reckless."

She locked eyes with me. The amber irises seemed to deepen, the pupils widening until the gold was just a thin, bright ring. I couldn't look away. I wasn't sure I was allowed to.

"So here's my offer."

The forest stood still. Every branch straining to listen, every leaf frozen mid-shiver, every shadow leaning in. The silence was so complete I could hear the blood rushing in my own ears, the soft creak of my leather gloves as my fists tightened, the faint hiss of frost sublimating off the branches into the cold night air.

"I will open the Void," she said. "I will break the prison holding Calum Ravenscroft."

I couldn't breathe. The air was there—I could feel it, cold against my lips—but my lungs refused to move. My ribs locked. The hope that had flared moments before was now a roaring thing, filling my chest cavity, crowding out everything else.

"But in exchange," and her voice dropped, soft and lethal, barely louder than a breath, intimate as a hand closing around a throat—

"I want something far more valuable than your life."

The words fell, cold as snow. They settled on my skin and didn't melt. I felt the weight of them—not metaphorical, but physical, a pressure across my shoulders, a heaviness in my hands.

The clearing waited.

"What do you want?" I asked.

My voice held. Barely.

Her smile widened. It stretched across her face, slow and sure and terrible, and the shadows behind her seemed to stretch with it, deepening, reaching, as though her smile had a shadow of its own.

"I want your story."

15

The words hung in the open air, brittle and sharp as frost. I watched Kakia, my mind numb and slow, the way a river moves under ice—still there, still turning, but trapped beneath something cold and thick. My fingers had gone bloodless at my sides. The taste of copper sat on the back of my tongue, thin and metallic, the aftertaste of too much adrenaline with nowhere to go.

"I don't understand," I said.

She looked at me, the glint in her eyes cold and bright, the pale grey of them catching the last weak light filtering through the canopy like coins at the bottom of a well. One corner of her mouth twitched—not quite a smile, not quite contempt. Something between the two, something that lived in the narrow space where patience meets hunger.

"That's because you're not thinking big enough."

The clearing was darker now; the trees leaned inward, their branches straining, hungry for what was about to unfold. Bark groaned softly as trunks shifted, the sound low and wet, like old bones settling. The moss beneath my boots had gone from soft and damp to something firmer, almost warm, as though the ground itself had begun to pulse. Somewhere in the canopy, a bird had been singing when I arrived. It was silent now. Everything was silent except for Kakia's voice and the faint hiss of wind threading through dead leaves.

"You expect me to ask for your life," she said. "That's what everyone thinks."

"And you don't?"

She almost smiled. The muscles around her jaw tightened, and the expression that crossed her face was brief and sharp—a flicker of something that might have been amusement in a creature capable of it. Her lips parted just enough to show the edge of her teeth, white and even and slightly too perfect, the way a predator's teeth always are.

"Lives are cheap."

She drew closer, her shadow bleeding out behind her, stretching long and dark across the clearing floor, pooling against the base of the nearest oak like something liquid. The hem of her cloak barely whispered against the frost-stiffened grass. She smelled of old parchment and something underneath it—something mineral and deep, like the air inside a cave that hasn't been opened in centuries.

"What matters is memory."

A sickness cut through my ribs, coiling there, tight and low and physical. My stomach clenched. The muscles along my sides drew in as though bracing for a blow. I pressed my nails into my palms—a small, sharp pain to anchor myself.

"What do you mean?"

"You want Calum Ravenscroft freed from the Void."

"Yes."

My voice came out steady. I was distantly surprised by that.

"You want him returned to this world."

"Yes."

"And you want him returned whole."

That word landed heavy. It dropped through the clearing like a stone through glass, and I felt the fracture of it in my sternum, felt the way it cracked open something I'd been trying very hard to keep sealed. *Whole.* Not broken. Not emptied. Not the hollow-eyed thing the Void made of the people it kept too long. My throat worked around a swallow I couldn't quite complete.

"Yes."

Kakia's smile sharpened. The skin around her eyes creased, and her pupils contracted—a quick, involuntary tightening, the way a hawk's eyes adjust when prey breaks from cover.

"That takes power."

"How much?"

She traced her fingers through the air; the clearing warped, shadows growing longer, the ground humming with her. Where her fingertips moved, the air rippled like heat off summer stone, and the darkness between the trees deepened from grey to black. The hum rose through the soles of my boots, vibrating up through my ankles and into the bones of my shins—a low, resonant frequency, like standing on the chest of something enormous and sleeping. The frost on the nearest branches began to melt, water droplets catching the strange half-light and running down the bark in thin, silver threads.

"Enough to shatter the rules of reality," she said. "The Void isn't just a prison. It's a wound in the world. A place for broken things the world wants to forget."

Her voice had changed. Dropped lower, gone quieter, the way people speak in temples and tombs—places where the walls remember. The air thickened around her words, and I could feel them settle against my skin like damp cloth, heavy and clinging.

"And you want me to tear it open."

"Yes."

She was delighted. It showed in the lift of her chin, in the way her shoulders drew back—a subtle straightening, the posture of someone who has just been handed exactly what they wanted. Her nostrils flared slightly, the way a wolf's do when it catches a scent on the wind. The grey of her eyes had gone almost luminous, bright with something fierce and acquisitive.

"That's ambitious."

"I'm not leaving without an answer."

"No," she agreed. "You aren't."

She circled me, slow as a clock's hand. I tracked her movement by sound—the soft crush of frost under her feet, the whisper of her cloak dragging through the dead grass. When she passed behind me, the skin along the back of my neck prickled, every small hair rising. The air she displaced was cold. Colder than the clearing. Colder than the frost. The kind of cold that doesn't come from weather but from absence—the temperature of a room after something vital has left it.

"The price I want is simple."

"I'm listening."

My jaw was tight. I could feel the tension in my molars, the dull ache of clenching.

"You give me your story."

Frustration stung, hot and bright behind my eyes. My hands twitched at my sides. "You've said that."

"And you still don't grasp it."

She stopped in front of me. Close enough that I could see the individual threads of silver woven through her dark hair, could see the faint lines etched around her mouth—not from age, but from centuries of smiling at the wrong things. Her breath misted between us, but only barely, as though even the cold wasn't sure how much of her was real.

"What is the greatest force in existence?" she asked.

"Magic."

"No."

"Love."

She shook her head. A single, precise movement, left to right. A teacher correcting a student. A surgeon adjusting a blade.

"Memory."

The word dropped like a stone into water. I felt the ripple of it move outward from the center of my chest, spreading through my ribs, my arms, my fingertips. The clearing seemed to absorb it. The trees creaked. The wind died.

"Stories shape the world," she said. "They make heroes and monsters."

Her gaze was sharper now, cutting through the dim light between us with surgical precision. She studied my face the way a jeweler studies a stone—looking for the fault line, the place where pressure would make it break clean.

"And you want to save your monster."

"Yes."

The word tasted like iron. Like blood bitten from the inside of my cheek.

"Then I'll take the story that made him one."

The meaning sank in, cold and slow, the way winter sinks into a lake—surface first, then deeper, then all the way down to the silt and the stones at the bottom where nothing moves.

"You want our history."

She nodded, pleased. Her chin dipped once, smooth and satisfied, and her fingers curled at her sides—a small, involuntary gesture of possession, like a hand closing around a key.

"But that's not all."

Her voice was soft, dangerous. The kind of quiet that comes before the ground gives way.

"When I take your story, Ottilie Valentine... the world will forget it."

A chill ran down my arms, prickling the skin from shoulder to wrist. The fine hairs rose. My breath caught somewhere between my lungs and my throat, trapped in the narrow passage of my windpipe like a bird against glass.

"Forget?"

"Every moment. Every kiss. Every promise."

The air pressed in, close as a hand on my throat. The trees seemed nearer than they'd been a moment ago. The canopy above had thickened, branches interlocking like fingers, and the last pale light was being slowly, steadily strangled. I could hear my own heartbeat now—a thick, wet sound, too loud in the quiet of the clearing, pulsing in my ears and at the base of my jaw.

"No one will remember what you were to him. Not the court. Not the gods. Not even history."

The words settled over me like snowfall—silent, relentless, covering everything.

I swallowed, trying to steady my voice. The muscles of my throat ached with the effort. "And Calum?"

Kakia considered me. Her head tilted a fraction to the left, her eyes tracking across my face with the slow, deliberate attention of someone reading very fine print. She took her time. She let the silence stretch until it hummed.

"That depends."

"On what?"

"How much of the story you keep for yourself."

My heart thudded. A single, hard beat that I felt in my wrists, my temples, the hollow of my throat. The clearing seemed to contract around it—the trees drawing in, the shadows deepening, the frost on the ground glittering sharper.

"You're asking me to erase myself."

"Yes."

"You're asking me to vanish."

She inclined her head. A slow, graceful tilt, like a candle flame bending in a draft.

Wind rattled in the branches overhead. Dry and sharp, scraping bark against bark, the sound of something restless moving through the canopy. A dead leaf spiraled down between us and landed on the frozen ground without a sound.

"What happens to me?" I said.

"You keep living."

"Just... invisible."

"Yes."

"No songs. No history. *No legacy.*"

It was a weight, real and cold. I could feel it settle across my shoulders, pressing down through my collarbones, compressing my lungs. The kind of weight that doesn't crush you all at once but slowly, over years, the way water wears through stone.

"You'll become a ghost," she said quietly. Her voice had lost its edge. What remained was something worse—something almost gentle, almost kind, the way a blade is gentle when it's sharp enough. "A life that happened, but left no mark."

"And Calum?"

"If you give me the whole story..."

She paused. Let the silence fill in the shape of what came next.

"He'll remember nothing of you."

The pain of it was sharp, clean as a knife. It entered between my ribs on the left side, precise and deep, and I felt my breath leave me in a single, involuntary exhale—not a gasp, not a cry, just the quiet sound of something being punctured. My vision blurred for a half-second. I blinked it clear.

"And if I don't?"

"If you keep a fragment..."

Her voice softened further, dropping to something barely above a whisper, intimate and terrible.

"He might remember something."

Not clear. Just a shadow. Enough to haunt him. A face he couldn't place. A name on the tip of his tongue that never quite arrived. The phantom ache of a wound he couldn't find on his body.

I tried to breathe. The air was thin and tasted of pine resin and something older—something that lived in the soil beneath the frost, in the roots of trees that had been growing since before the courts had names.

"You're cruel."

"Practical."

"You want me to destroy all evidence we existed."

She smiled, thin and bright, the expression pulling the skin taut across her cheekbones. "I want to know how badly you want him back."

The silence in the clearing felt almost alive. It had texture—a thickness, a presence, the way fog has presence. It pressed against my eardrums. I could feel it on my skin, cool and faintly electric, like the moment before lightning finds the ground.

"Will he live?"

"Yes."

"Will he escape the Void?"

"Yes."

"Will he survive?"

"Yes."

"And the price is my story."

"Yes."

It should have been impossible. It wasn't.

Because Calum had already spent everything for me. The least I could do was vanish.

"I accept," I said.

My voice didn't shake. I was grateful for that.

Kakia's smile was triumphant. It broke across her face like dawn—slow and inevitable and illuminating things that had been hiding in the dark. Her eyes widened fractionally, her pupils expanding, black swallowing grey, and for a single heartbeat she looked almost beautiful in the way that terrible things sometimes are.

"I thought you might."

The clearing changed. The ground split in a slow, deliberate ring, cracks radiating outward from where I stood like veins in marble, and light burned up from old symbols scored into the earth—symbols I didn't recognize, carved in a language that predated the fae, predated the courts, predated everything I had ever been taught to name. The light was amber and gold and something else, something that had no color I could identify, something that sat at the edge of perception and hummed against the backs of my eyes. The air smelled of old blood and the sweet, decaying scent of flowers left too long in water.

"Stand inside," she said.

I stepped forward. My boots crossed the threshold of the outermost ring, and the ground beneath me vibrated—a deep, subsonic tremor that I felt in my teeth, in the joints of my knees, in the base of my skull.

Cold magic climbed my ankles. It moved like water but felt nothing like it—denser, slower, with a viscosity that pulled at my skin. The sensation was not painful. It was worse than painful. It was the feeling of something being gently, carefully removed, the way a surgeon lifts a splinter from beneath the nail.

"What now?" I asked.

"Give me the story."

"How?"

"Tell it."

The words echoed, strange and sharp, bouncing off the trees and the frozen air and the walls of the ritual circle as though the clearing had suddenly developed acoustics it hadn't possessed before. The echo layered over itself—*tell it, tell it, tell it*—each repetition thinner, higher, until it dissolved into a frequency I could feel but no longer hear.

"What?"

"Every moment," she said. "The beginning. The middle. The end."

My throat tried to close. The muscles along the sides of my neck seized, and I tasted salt—tears or fear, I couldn't tell which. My tongue pressed against the roof of my mouth, dry and heavy. But I spoke.

I told her about the ball.

The way the light had fallen through the glass ceiling of the Solstice Hall in long, golden shafts that turned the dust motes into constellations.

The way the music had changed when he entered—not literally, but something in the air had shifted, some invisible frequency that made the hairs on my arms stand up and my breath catch in my chest before I'd even turned to see him.

The balcony. Cold stone under my palms. The smell of night-blooming jasmine rising from the gardens below. His voice behind me—low, careful, the way you speak to something wild that might bolt. The way my heart had hammered so hard I was certain he could hear it.

The willow tree. Its branches trailing in the dark water of

the reflecting pool, creating curtains of pale green that whispered when the wind moved through them. His hand finding mine beneath the leaves. The shock of his skin—warmer than I'd expected, rougher, the calluses on his fingers catching against the soft inside of my wrist.

Secret meetings under the moon. The taste of stolen wine. The way he laughed—rare and startled, as though the sound surprised him as much as it surprised me. The weight of his coat around my shoulders on cold nights when I'd come to the garden wall without one.

The first kiss. The way his hand had trembled against my jaw. The way my breath had stopped, simply stopped, the way a clock stops when you reach inside and still the pendulum. The taste of him—smoke and winter apples and something darker, something that lived beneath the surface of his careful restraint.

Promises in quiet gardens. Whispered words that tasted like treason. Plans sketched in the margins of stolen hours. The feeling of his forehead pressed against mine in the dark, both of us breathing the same thin air, both of us knowing what we were building and what it would cost.

Every memory.

And with every word, the magic took them.

I felt each one leave—a small, specific loss, like pulling threads from a tapestry.

The color drained first. Then the texture. Then the shape.

The memory of the ball became flat and grey, then transparent, then nothing. The balcony dissolved. The willow tree. His laugh. The weight of his coat. One by one, they lifted from the place inside my chest where I had kept them and rose into the air of the clearing, shimmering and translucent, turning slowly like leaves caught in an updraft.

The clearing filled with shifting light; memories rose up,

burning away into the air. They caught fire at the edges—a pale, white flame that consumed them silently, without heat, without sound, leaving only a faint shimmer that dissipated into the dark. The warmth in my chest faded, piece by piece, like a fire burning down room by room through a house I'd lived in my whole life. Doors closing. Lights going out. Hallways going dark.

Until only one memory remained.

Small. Stubborn. Buried so deep that the magic had to reach for it and couldn't quite close its fingers around it. A single moment—his face in the grey light before dawn, turned toward me on the pillow, his eyes still closed, his breathing slow and even, and the way my chest had ached with a love so enormous it felt like drowning. Not the kiss. Not the promise. Just his sleeping face. Just the quiet.

Kakia noticed.

Her gaze dropped to my chest, to the place where the last ember of warmth still pulsed, faint and defiant. Her nostrils flared. Her fingers twitched at her sides.

"You're keeping something."

"Yes."

Her eyes narrowed. The lines around them deepened, and her jaw tightened—a brief flash of something that might have been irritation, might have been respect.

"They always do."

I closed my eyes. The darkness behind my lids was vast and empty, scraped clean, and the single remaining memory burned there like a distant star in a sky where every other light had been extinguished.

"It's enough."

She watched me for a long time. I felt her gaze on my face like pressure, like the weight of a hand hovering just above the skin. The clearing was silent. The ritual circle hummed softly beneath my feet, patient and waiting. Frost crept along the edges of the carved symbols, delicate and precise, tracing the ancient lines in white.

Then she smiled, slow and certain. The expression moved across her face like a tide coming in—inevitable, unhurried, covering everything.

"Very well."

She raised her hands. Her fingers spread wide, pale against the dark, and the tendons in her wrists stood out like cables. The air between her palms thickened, went dark, then ignited.

The ritual circle detonated with light; ancient power roared into the sky. The sound was not a sound—it was a pressure, a force, a concussive wave that flattened the grass and bent the trees outward and drove the breath from my lungs. The light was blinding, white and gold and that nameless color again, pouring upward in a column that split the canopy and pierced the clouds and kept going—up and up and up, until it was a needle of brilliance punching through the fabric of the sky itself.

The ground shook. The trees groaned. The frost on every surface vaporized in an instant, filling the clearing with a thin, cold mist that tasted of salt and stone and something ancient and electrical.

Far beyond the Seelie woods, beyond the realms of gods and fae, a crack split the endless dark of the Void.

Not a metaphor. An actual crack—a fracture in the black, a seam of white-gold light splitting the nothing like a wound opening in skin. The sound it made was the sound of the world remembering a door it had sealed shut. The sound of a lock being broken from the outside.

And inside that prison—

Calum Ravenscroft felt it.

The first fracture. The first hint of escape.

A tremor that moved through the formless dark like a heartbeat. A warmth against his skin that he hadn't felt in— how long? How long had it been? He couldn't remember. The Void had eaten his sense of time the way it ate everything else. But this—this warmth. This light. It felt like—

Something. Someone.

A name he almost knew.

And the echo of a story the world was already starting to forget.

The magic faded slowly.

Not like an explosion.

Not like a storm.

But like a candle burning down to its last thread—the flame shrinking, the wax pooling, the light narrowing to a single trembling point that clung to existence through stubbornness alone before finally, quietly, letting go.

The ritual circle beneath my feet dimmed one symbol at a time, the old runes sinking back into the forest floor as the power spent itself. Each one guttered like an ember drowning in ash—amber to rust to grey to nothing. The carved lines in the earth filled with frost again, slowly, the ice creeping in to reclaim what the magic had scorched clean. The air grew lighter with each breath, the pressure of the spell lifting from the clearing like a hand being removed from the surface of water, and the world rushed in to fill the space it left behind.

When the last sigil went dark, the forest returned.

Wind moved through the branches—tentative at first, then

stronger, as though the trees were exhaling after holding their breath for a very long time.

Frost glittered along the leaves, catching the thin moonlight that filtered back through the canopy in pale, fractured shards.

An owl called, somewhere distant. A fox moved through the undergrowth, its footsteps crunching softly over frozen leaves.

The world continued as if nothing had changed.

But something had.

I could feel it.

A hollow space inside my chest, like something vital had been cut away. Not painful—not exactly. More like the absence of pain. The phantom ache of a limb that's already been removed, the nerve endings still firing into empty air, still reaching for something that isn't there anymore. I pressed my hand flat against my sternum. The skin was cold through the fabric of my shirt. Beneath it, my heart beat steadily, evenly, as though nothing had happened. As though the emptiness wasn't real.

But my hand knew. My hand could feel the difference—the way the rhythm had changed, gone thinner, gone quieter, like music playing in a room that's suddenly too large.

Across the clearing, Kakia watched me with quiet interest. She stood very still, her hands folded in front of her, her head tilted at that precise, predatory angle. The ritual's light had left a faint phosphorescence on her skin—a pale shimmer along her cheekbones and the bridge of her nose that faded as I watched, sinking into her like water into dry earth. She looked fed. Satisfied. The hollows beneath her eyes had filled in, and the sharp angles of her face had softened almost imperceptibly, as though whatever she had taken from me had substance and weight and she had consumed it.

"It's done," she said.

My voice felt thin. Stretched. Like fabric worn too many times, the threads pulling apart at the weave. "He's free?"

"Not yet."

The answer landed heavier than I'd expected. My knees almost buckled. I locked them, stiffened my spine, pressed my feet harder into the frozen ground. The cold seeped through the soles of my boots and into the arches of my feet, grounding me.

"But the prison is broken," she said. "The Void has cracked."

"How long until he escapes?"

Kakia smiled faintly. The expression barely moved her mouth—just a slight upward pull at the corners, a suggestion of amusement that didn't reach her eyes.

"That depends on how stubborn he is."

"That's not reassuring."

"It's accurate."

I nodded, slow. The motion felt heavy, as though my head had gained weight.

Calum had always been stubborn. Stubborn the way stone is stubborn—not through effort, but through nature. Through the simple, immovable fact of what he was. He had been stubborn when the courts condemned him. Stubborn when the gods turned their backs. Stubborn when the Void swallowed him whole and the world above sealed the wound and pretended he had never existed.

That thought steadied me. I held onto it the way a drowning person holds onto wreckage—not gracefully, not with dignity, but with everything I had.

"He'll survive," I said softly.

"Yes."

"And he'll come back."

"Yes."

The hollow inside my chest tightened. The edges of the empty space contracted, pulling at the surrounding tissue like a wound trying to close around something that wasn't there. My breath hitched. I pressed my palm harder against my sternum.

"And he won't remember me."

Kakia's smile widened.

"Oh no," she said, gentle as a knife—the kind of gentleness that draws blood so cleanly you don't feel it until you look down and see the red.

"That part isn't true at all."

My frown was slow, dragging, the muscles of my face responding as though through deep water. "You said—"

"I said I wanted your story."

"You did."

"And I gave it to you."

"Yes."

"But you misunderstood something."

The forest seemed to draw in, cold and tight. The trees pressed closer—not moving, not physically, but the shadows between them deepened and the spaces narrowed and the air thickened until the clearing felt less like an opening in the woods and more like a room. A room that was getting smaller.

"What do you mean?"

Kakia stepped closer. Her boots made no sound on the frozen ground. She moved the way smoke moves—fluid, unhurried, filling whatever space was available. The phosphorescent shimmer on her skin had faded completely, but something else had replaced it—a warmth, a vitality, a brightness in her grey eyes that hadn't been there before. She looked younger. Stronger. More present, as though she had been slightly translucent before and was now fully, terribly solid.

"You assumed taking your story meant erasing it."

"That's what you said."

"No," she replied, voice soft. The word was barely a breath. A whisper that carried further than it should have, reaching the edges of the clearing and echoing back, layered and strange.

"That's what you thought."

My stomach twisted. A physical sensation—a clenching, a turning, the muscles of my abdomen contracting around a knot of cold that had nothing to do with the frost.

"What did you actually take?"

Kakia's eyes gleamed. The grey of them caught the moonlight and held it, refracting it into something sharper, something with an edge.

"Stories are powerful things, Ottilie Valentine. They shape worlds. They haunt people. They change the course of history."

Her voice was low, each sentence landing with the weight of a stone being placed on a scale. The air around her words thickened, grew heavy, and I could smell something new beneath the pine and frost—ink. Old ink. The kind that stains fingers and never fully washes out. The kind that lives in the spines of books that have been read so many times the pages have gone soft.

"And yours... is extraordinary."

The wind moved through the trees, carrying with it the faint, distant sound of water running beneath ice—a muffled, persistent rushing, like blood through veins.

"You and Calum Ravenscroft," she said, quiet. Almost reverent. Almost hungry.

"A fae princess and a god of nightmares. A love story that started a war."

Her smile sharpened. The teeth showed again—white, even, precise.

"Why would I erase something that valuable?"

A chill crept into my bones. Not the surface cold of frost and winter air, but something deeper—a cold that started in the marrow and worked outward, radiating through the bone into the muscle, into the skin. The kind of cold that doesn't respond to warmth. The kind that stays.

"What did you do?"

"I claimed it."

The clearing tilted, just a little. The ground beneath my feet shifted—not physically, not measurably, but some internal axis recalibrated, and the world went briefly sideways before righting itself. I swayed. Caught my balance. My fingers found the rough bark of the nearest tree and gripped it, the texture biting into my palm—real, solid, something to hold onto.

"Claimed?"

"Yes."

She gestured at the fading ritual circle. The last traces of light were nearly gone now—just faint lines of amber glowing in the carved earth, thin as thread, pulsing weakly like the final heartbeats of something dying.

"That story belongs to me now."

I stared at her. My eyes burned. I realized I hadn't blinked in too long, and when I did, the moisture that rushed in was sharp and stinging.

"You said the world would forget."

"I said the story would be mine."

"That's not the same thing."

"No," she agreed. Her voice was light. Conversational. The tone of someone discussing the weather or the price of grain.

"It isn't."

Cold dread began to pool inside me. It gathered in the hollow space where my memories had been, filling the empti-ness with something worse than emptiness—a thick, viscous understanding that rose slowly, like floodwater in a cellar, dark and patient and inevitable.

"What happens to me?" I asked.

Kakia tipped her head, studying me. Her gaze moved across my face the way a sculptor's hands move across clay—assessing structure, looking for the places where the material would yield. Her lips parted slightly. Her tongue touched the corner of her mouth—a quick, unconscious gesture, the way someone licks their lips before a meal.

"*You* become the story."

The words struck like a drop in temperature—sudden, total, the kind of cold that makes you gasp before you understand why. My skin contracted. My lungs seized. The air in my throat crystallized into something sharp and thin.

"I don't understand."

"You will."

The forest shifted. The clearing darkened, shadows gathering thick and fast, pooling along the ground like spilled ink. They moved with purpose—flowing toward the center of the clearing, toward me, toward the fading ritual circle, collecting in the carved lines and filling them with darkness instead of light. The smell of old ink intensified, mixing with something else now—something sweet and cloying, like overripe fruit, like honey left to ferment. The sound of the wind changed. It was no longer moving through the branches. It was moving through something else—something hollow, something resonant, producing a low, continuous tone that vibrated in my chest.

"You asked what happens now," she said.

"Now you come with me."

My pulse spiked. The blood surged through my veins so fast I could feel it in my fingertips, in the thin skin behind my ears, in the soft tissue of my throat. My body understood before my mind did—muscles tensing, weight shifting to the balls of my feet, every survival instinct I'd ever possessed snapping to attention at once.

"No."

"Yes."

I stepped back. My heel caught on a root, and I stumbled—just a half-step, just enough to break my stance—before catching myself. The bark of the tree behind me pressed into my shoulder blade through my shirt, rough and cold and real.

"That wasn't part of the bargain."

"Oh, it absolutely was."

"You never said—"

"I never said you would leave."

The realization struck, hard and final. It hit the way the ground hits when you fall from a great height—not gradually, not with warning, but all at once, the full force of it arriving in a single instant that compresses everything into a point of impact so dense it stops time.

I had been careful. I had listened to every word. I had weighed each sentence, tested each clause, searched for the trap the way you search for the needle in the dark. And I had missed it. Not because it was hidden. Because it was *absent*. She hadn't said I would leave. She hadn't said I would be free. She hadn't said any of it, and I had filled the silence with my own assumptions and built a bridge out of nothing and walked across it.

"You tricked me."

Kakia laughed, low and bright. The sound rang through the clearing like a bell—clear and musical and fundamentally wrong, the way a beautiful sound is wrong when it comes from the mouth of something that shouldn't be capable of beauty.

Her head tipped back. The column of her throat gleamed

pale in the moonlight. Her shoulders shook with genuine, unguarded delight.

"Of course I did."

The shadows crowded the clearing. They pressed in from every side, dense and deliberate, and the trees beyond them vanished—swallowed into a darkness so complete it looked solid. The clearing was shrinking. The world was shrinking. The moonlight overhead dimmed to a thin, grey wash, and the frost on the ground turned black, as though the cold itself had changed color.

"Stories need witnesses," she said. Her voice had dropped again—low, intimate, conspiratorial. The voice of someone sharing a secret they've kept for a very long time.

"They need something to anchor them. And you, my dear princess, are the perfect anchor."

The ground beneath my feet shifted. A sound—deep, geological, the groan of stone being forced apart by something patient and enormous—rose from below. Cracks spread outward from the center of the dead ritual circle, and the earth split along them, opening like a wound, revealing stone steps that curved downward in a tight, deliberate spiral.

The steps were old. Older than the forest. Older than the symbols that had been carved into the ground above them. They were made of a grey stone I didn't recognize—smooth, almost glassy, shot through with veins of something dark that caught the fading light and held it.

Cold air rose from the dark below, carrying with it the smell of deep earth and still water and the faint, papery scent of very old books.

"You're imprisoning me."

"Yes."

"You said I would live."

"And you will."

My heart pounded. Each beat was a concussion in my chest, violent and distinct, shaking the hollow space where my memories had been.

"For how long?"

Kakia smiled.

"As long as the story lasts."

"And how long is that?"

She leaned in, close. Close enough that I could see the individual flecks of silver in her grey eyes. Close enough that her breath touched my face—cold, faintly sweet, carrying that scent of old ink and older things. Close enough that I could see the way her pupils had expanded until the grey was just a thin ring around an abyss of black.

"Oh, Ottilie. Your story will never die."

It hit like thunder. The understanding arrived all at once—not piece by piece, not gradually, but in a single, devastating wave that crashed through the hollow in my chest and filled it with something colder than emptiness. Colder than grief. The cold of permanence. The cold of *forever*.

"You're going to tell it."

"To whom?"

"Everyone."

Her eyes were bright with delight. They shone in the darkness of the closing clearing like two points of pale fire, and her face was luminous with the particular joy of someone who has just acquired something irreplaceable.

"The world will remember you. The fae princess who loved a monster. The woman who caused a god to slaughter an entire court. Songs will be written. Legends will spread. Your name will echo through centuries."

Each sentence landed like a nail being driven into wood—precise, deliberate, final. My name. My story. Not erased. Preserved. Kept. Owned. Told and retold by a creature who would shape it however she pleased, who would bend it and polish it and sharpen it into whatever weapon served her best.

A sound escaped me—small, involuntary, not quite a gasp and not quite a sob. Something between the two. Something that had no name.

"And Calum?"

Kakia's smile was all teeth. Every one of them visible. The expression had abandoned any pretense of warmth or humanity and become what it had always been—the bared jaw of a predator displaying its instruments.

"He will remember you most of all."

Hope sparked, faint but real. A single ember in the vast, cold dark of the hollow inside me. It caught and held, trembling, fragile as a flame in wind.

"He'll come for me."

"Yes." Her voice was almost amused. A low, warm sound, the sound of someone settling into a chair by a fire, comfortable and entertained. The sound of someone who knows exactly how the story ends.

"That's the best part."

"What do you mean?"

She gestured at the dark stairway yawning open beneath the forest. The steps spiraled down and down, curving out of sight, and the darkness below was absolute—not the absence of light but the presence of something else, something thick and textured that seemed to breathe.

"Monsters are very good at destroying the world for the people they love."

The ground trembled, faintly. A vibration that started deep below the surface and rose through the stone steps and the frozen earth and the roots of the ancient trees. The branches above shook. A shower of frost crystals fell through the air, catching the last traces of light as they descended, glittering like shattered glass.

Far away.

Beyond the forest.

Beyond the sky.

The Void shuddered. The crack that the ritual had opened widened by a fraction—a hair's width, no more—and the white-gold light that bled through it pulsed once, strong and steady, like a heartbeat finding its rhythm.

Kakia's eyes flicked upward. Her smile faltered for the first time—not disappearing, but shifting, tightening at the edges, gaining a new quality. Anticipation. The look of someone who has just heard the first distant rumble of a storm they've been waiting for.

"It's already beginning."

My pulse raced. Blood roared in my ears.

"He's breaking the prison."

"Yes."

"And when he escapes…"

Her smile widened. It spread slowly, deliberately, like a crack spreading through ice—inevitable, irreversible, beautiful in the way that destruction is sometimes beautiful.

"…he will search for you."

Cold understanding swept over me. It moved through my body like a tide—starting at the crown of my head and flowing downward, through my face, my throat, my chest, my stomach, my legs, my feet, until every part of me was submerged in it. The understanding was simple. The understanding was perfect. The understanding was the cruelest thing she had done to me yet.

He would search. He would remember my face, my name, the shape of what we'd been. He would carry the story she told him—the story she now owned—and he would follow it like a map. But the map would lead nowhere. The map would lead everywhere. The map would lead him through centuries of searching, through kingdoms and ruins and the wreckage of his own rage, and he would never arrive.

"He'll never find me."

"No."

"But he will keep trying."

She stepped aside, revealing the stairway spiraling into darkness. The gesture was almost courteous—a host showing a guest to their room. Her arm extended, palm up, fingers slightly curved, the posture of someone who has all the time in the world and knows it.

"You will live here," she said. "Where stories are kept. Where bargains are remembered."

The air rising from below was cold and still and smelled of stone and silence. Not the silence of an empty room but the silence of a library after closing—a silence that contained things, that held them, that kept them preserved in the amber of its own stillness.

Cold dread settled in my bones. It found the marrow and made itself at home, curling into the spaces between the cells, weaving itself into the structure of me. It would live there now. It would always live there.

"Why?"

"Because tragedy is the most powerful story of all."

The forest above faded, distant and unreachable. The canopy had sealed itself—branches woven tight as a basket, leaves layered thick as thatch, and the moonlight that had filtered through was gone. The clearing existed now in a permanent twilight, lit only by the faint, residual glow of the dead ritual circle and the pale luminescence of Kakia's eyes.

"You will watch the centuries pass," Kakia said. "You will

watch your legend grow. And you will watch the monster you loved tear the world apart trying to reach you."

Her voice was quiet. Almost tender. The tenderness of someone who genuinely appreciates the value of what they've taken.

My hands shook. I looked down at them—my own hands, pale and trembling in the half-light, the knuckles white, the fingers curled inward like the petals of a flower closing against the cold. They didn't look like the hands of a princess. They looked like the hands of someone who has just realized the size of the cage they've walked into.

"You're cruel."

"I'm a collector."

The darkness below the steps was endless. It didn't invite. It didn't threaten. It simply waited, with the patience of something that has never had to hurry, that has never been refused, that knows with absolute certainty that everything eventually comes down.

"Come," she said.

I hesitated, just once.

My feet stopped at the edge of the first step. The stone was smooth beneath my boot—cold through the leather, polished by centuries of descent. The air from below moved against my face, stirring the loose strands of hair at my temples, carrying that scent of old books and older silence. I closed my eyes.

Behind my lids, the single remaining memory burned. His sleeping face. The grey light of dawn. The slow rise and fall of his chest. The way my heart had felt too large for my body, too full, too heavy with the weight of loving something the world had decided was unforgivable.

I held it. Pressed it tight against the inside of my ribs, where the hollow was deepest.

Because somewhere under the fear, hope still burned.

Calum would break the Void.

He would. The way he broke everything—thoroughly, completely, with the full devastating force of what he was. He would shatter it the way he had shattered the Autumn Court. The way he had shattered the laws of gods and the expectations of centuries and every cage anyone had ever tried to build around him.

And when he did—the world would tremble.

I opened my eyes. Kakia was watching me with an expression I hadn't seen before—something quiet, something almost like respect. It passed quickly. It was replaced by the smile.

I stepped toward the stairs.

The first step was cold. The second was colder. By the third, the temperature of the air had dropped so far that my breath came out in thick, white plumes that hung motionless in the still air before dissolving. The spiral tightened. The walls of the stairwell—rough stone, damp with condensation, slick with something that might have been moss and might have been something older—closed in around me. The light from above narrowed to a thin, grey disc that shrank with every step.

Behind me, Kakia's footsteps followed. Soft. Measured. Patient.

Behind us, the forest sealed itself closed. The earth drew together over the stairway like a wound healing—soil and root and frost and stone, folding inward, compressing, until the clearing above was whole again. Unmarked. Unbroken. A patch of frozen forest floor indistinguishable from any other.

The owl called again, distant and unconcerned.

The fox moved on.

The wind continued through the trees.

And below the ground, in the darkness where stories are

kept, where bargains are remembered, where the echoes of extraordinary things are preserved in silence and shadow and the endless, patient architecture of forever—the story began.

I love you, Calum Ravenscroft.

AFTERWORD

If this book hurt you a little, I'm sorry. And I mean that in the most genuine way—because if you felt something break while reading this, if you had to pause and stare at the wall for a minute, if a line hit a little too close to something you've lived through, I see you.

This story was never meant to be easy. It was meant to feel real. And sometimes real love isn't soft or safe or fair—it's messy, consuming, and it leaves marks. If you've ever loved someone who couldn't love you back the way you needed, if you've ever held on longer than you should have, if you've ever had to walk away from something that felt like it could have been everything—You're not alone. And I'm really grateful you trusted this story enough to feel it.

Thank you for loving these characters, even when it hurt. Thank you for staying. Take care of your heart after this one. You deserve that.

Don't forget to leave a review!
www.ryenwrites.io
@ryenwrites

ACKNOWLEDGMENTS

This book was written in fragments as I definitely don't write in ideal conditions haha. I write tired, I write between meals, during sick days, teething, after therapy... you get the gist, its in fulllllll survival mode.

To my children, you will never remember the versions of me that wrote this book, but you are the reason I keep going, even on the days it feels impossible. I hope I make you proud.

To my readers, thank you for meeting me here. For choosing stories that don't resolve cleanly. For loving characters who make terrible choices for the right(ish) reasons. For letting something dark, strange, and a little unhinged take up space in your life.

And to the version of me who wrote this in the margins of everything else. You did it!! This series exists because you refused to wait for the perfect moment.

— Ryen Santana

ABOUT THE AUTHOR

Ryen Santana is an author who has spent her life weaving stories—first in the world of fanfiction and now in dark, emotionally charged novels. A mother of two, she balances the chaos of parenthood with the equally chaotic process of crafting narratives filled with morally grey characters, deep betrayals, and enough trauma to keep her readers up at night.

Her love for storytelling began in her early teens, where she honed her skills writing sprawling, 500k+ word fanfics inspired by Twilight, The Hunger Games, Divergent, and, of course, One Direction. If a fandom existed, she either wrote for it or devoured every story it had to offer.

When she's not writing, she can be found indulging in her other passions—reading (obviously), rock climbing, spending all of the money she earns from books on commissioning art of her characters, and consuming unhealthy amounts of caffeine. She also enjoys rotting in bed whenever life allows, though with two small children, those moments are rare and precious.

Now, with her original works, she continues to explore the themes that first captivated her: love, power, revenge, and the darker sides of human nature. But this time, the stakes are higher, the characters more twisted, and the endings never quite what you expect.

instagram.com/ryenwrites

www.ingramcontent.com/pod-product-compliance
Lightning Source LLC
Chambersburg PA
CBHW032020150726
47990CB00005B/2053